"We're leaving."

Her words had an edge to them, and her face was creased with worry.

"Dr. Drager, please, what is going on?"

"Ashley... You might as well call me by my first name. I'm essentially kidnapping you."

She transferred him to the wheelchair, and he waited for the dizziness to pass. "If I'm going to allow myself to be kidnapped, I need to know why."

"Something weird is going on here. You show up, beaten, with amnesia and a photo of me in your pocket. And your tattoo is the same exact one my father has, who's been missing. Then my father's arch-nemesis shows up looking for you..."

He got it. She thought he could provide her with answers. Maybe, too, she was the key to him getting his memory back.

"If we get out of here," he said, "what exactly is your plan?"

"To keep you a

Jordyn Redwood is a pediatric ER nurse by day, suspense novelist by night. She pursued her dream of becoming an author by first penning her medical thrillers *Proof, Poison* and *Peril*. Jordyn hosts *Redwood's Medical Edge*, a blog helping authors write medically accurate fiction. Living near the Rocky Mountains with her husband, two beautiful daughters and one crazy dog provides inspiration for her books. She loves to get email from her readers at jredwood1@gmail.com.

Books by Jordyn Redwood

Love Inspired Suspense

Fractured Memory
Taken Hostage
Fugitive Spy

FUGITIVE SPY

JORDYN REDWOOD

HARLEQUIN LOVE INSPIRED SUSPENSE

Recycling programs
for this product may
not exist in your area.

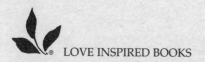

LOVE INSPIRED BOOKS

ISBN-13: 978-1-335-49027-8

Fugitive Spy

www.Harlequin.com

Printed in U.S.A.

And we know that all things work together for good
to them that love God, to them who are the called
according to his purpose.
—Romans 8:28

For Carolyn Mai: loving grandmother, fellow wordsmith, lover of books and knowledge. Thank you for passing on your passion for Christ and writing to me.

ONE

As CIA spy Casper English crossed the threshold into the abandoned home, the faint wheezes of a man teetering on death whispered just above the gusting snowstorm. Drawing his weapon, he inched farther into the darkness. A cast of faint moonlight illuminated an arm, seemingly disembodied, lying on the floor across the threshold of a doorway. The wind battered against the house so badly that the old wood walls groaned in distress.

Walking quickly, Casper closed the distance.

It was his partner, Ethan.

"You…found me."

Ethan's breaths came quick and ineffective. Casper's heartbeat quickened with each shallow gasp his partner… his friend…puffed out in vapors into the frigid night. Dark, thick fluid glistened from a wound in his chest, and Casper knelt down beside him to assess it. From an inner pocket of his leather jacket, Casper withdrew a small flashlight. Ethan's hand flew up and knocked it out before Casper could turn it on.

"They're…close. Too…close."

Instinctively, Casper rose up and looked out into the darkness through the fractured, dust-crusted glass of the nearest window. This location was too close to the city. To everything. Too hard to keep hidden from those who had chased Ethan. It was more likely than not that they were going to be discovered. How Ethan had crawled through snow to even hide here was unfathomable. Casper concentrated on the landscape. The trees threw thorny shadows onto the silky white drifts. Nothing moved that resembled a human. Ethan pulled something from his pocket. His hand lifted up and flopped against Casper's chest.

"Take them."

Casper grabbed the two items. A photo and a small piece of paper. In the darkness, he couldn't make out the information they contained. "Ethan, the terrorist attack. Did you find out anything about the date? The location?"

A faint shake of his head. Casper's stomach plummeted. None of this was good. His partner wasn't going to survive, the gathering darkness brooding in Ethan's eyes showed the shadow of the grim reaper on the hunt. Casper had seen it before in too many patients as they left this existence.

"The attack…is ES1…"

Casper swayed a bit at Ethan's revelation.

No, that's not possible. Does Ethan even know what he's saying? Or is his brain malfunctioning from blood loss?

"It…exists."

Ethan's eyes closed. Casper shook him by the shoulders and Ethan's head lolled to the side. He had to verify this information. If he took what Ethan said to his superiors without proof, they'd laugh him right out of the CIA. That was how crazy Ethan's statement was. Casper settled his hand in the center of Ethan's chest. The tension in Casper's gut eased as he felt it rise under his touch.

How was Ethan's claim possible? ES1 had been a theorized virus that combined two of the deadliest pathogens known to man—smallpox and Ebola. The Soviets reportedly looked to develop it before their illegal bioweapons program was discovered during a US inspection over twenty-five years ago. Purportedly, they'd abandoned their aspirations when the manufacturing sites had been dismantled.

Ethan's eyes fluttered open. "His daughter."

"Ashley," Casper confirmed.

Ethan nodded. "He...sent her..."

"What?"

"Information."

A spy sending sensitive information to a civilian? His own daughter? That didn't make sense to Casper. Dr. Russell Drager, a leading bioweapons specialist, had been missing for more than two years. Ethan and Casper had been tasked to find him before he fell into the wrong hands or was assassinated for his work for the CIA. How could a man, his mentor, endanger his daughter so easily? It spoke of desperation. Of not being able to trust those he reported to. If Russell had information concerning this pathogen, he needed to give it to his handler, Jared Fleming. The only reason Casper could imagine Russell taking such a risk was if he didn't trust Fleming anymore and didn't know who else Fleming might have corrupted.

"Fleming..." Ethan shook his head and clenched his hands against the wound, gritting his teeth together against the pain. A shudder ran through his body. "Compromised."

Casper's stomach knotted. How did that happen? A handler compromised? Russell told Casper once during his fellowship, rather flippantly, that ES1 would make Marburg look like the common cold if it were developed and released.

Had that been a warning for Casper? Did Russell know ES1 existed when he made that statement?

"Does Fleming know about Ashley? That she might have this information?" Casper asked.

"Hid it…from him."

"You were trying to find her?"

"Hospital. Close."

That was Castle Peak Medical Center. No wonder Ethan was in this area. He'd gotten this far before he was discovered trying to get Ashley—to protect her.

Will she even remember me? It's been years. We're both older. Different.

"Take her…address. Help."

Casper shoved the items into his partner's jeans pocket. He reached under his partner's shoulders to lift him up, assuming his words were meant for assistance, but Ethan was dead weight. Casper settled him back down and placed his cheek next to his lips.

Stillness. No inhalation. No exhalation.

Ethan was dead.

Clenching his hand into a fist, Casper punched the rotting wood planks. A window shattered and Casper instinctively flattened himself against the floor, his muscles tense. Even though his heart was heavy, there was no time for goodbyes. The decrepit back door whined as it shifted on its hinges, and Casper beelined through it and back out into the bitter night air.

As he ran, Casper tripped on a roving tree root and fell into the snow just as a bullet whizzed past his ear, the high-pitched whine adding more chill to his bones than the drift he'd face-planted in. He wiped the frozen crystals from his eyes and tried to get his bearings. He needed a place to hide. There was a four-lane road off to his right. Cars streamed by and he considered commandeering one, but discarded the thought as it would draw too much attention.

If he didn't move fast, they were going to catch him and he wouldn't be able to find Ashley and safeguard her.

On his left, there was a copse of timber skeletons. In the faint moonlight, he couldn't see the depth of them, but they were his only option for cover. The sound of heavy boot falls brought him to his feet and he ran, reaching instinctively to the waistband of his jeans for the small firearm he'd stowed there.

It was gone. Likely ejected from its spot into the snow when he fell.

Just as Casper reached a running stride, a hand clasped his shoulder and his feet tangled underneath him. A man, taller and heavier, forced him over onto his back. Two of his cohorts closed the remaining gap, each taking several swift kicks into his rib cage and sternum. His lungs exploded in white-hot fire. He tried to breathe. The effect of those blows was the same as being dropped straight onto his back and getting the wind knocked out of him. There was a glint of a knife straight up his jacket and shirt, the fabric falling away from his chest. Rough hands patted his body, his pants pocket. A fist connected with his jaw and his head spun.

They were going to kill him.

"Where is it?" one of the men yelled, delivering another kick to the side of his head.

Casper flipped over and staggered onto his hands and knees. Droplets of blood—his blood—darkened the snow. A cut to his forehead? Pain seared in his chest as he coaxed the freezing air in.

He didn't know what they wanted, and if they determined he didn't have it…they'd kill him just like Ethan.

"Mr. English, if we don't get the thumb drive, not

only will you die, but whoever has it will suffer the same fate as you."

If Casper admitted he didn't know what they were talking about, they'd finish him off without a thought. Ashley would be next. Would she even survive the night?

Pain exploded as something unyielding connected with the back of his head. He splayed out onto the ground. Was someone whistling? A dog barking?

Blackness.

The unconscious man was going to die if ER physician Ashley Drager didn't do something.

Quickly.

"Ashley, his heart is throwing off some bad beats," said Lance, one of the ER nurses, a raised urgency to his voice.

Ashley glanced at the monitor. The rogue missteps of their patient's heart had traversed by, now only witnessed by the ECG tracing the monitor automatically printed. His heart rate was on the low side, but considering his seemingly excellent physical shape that could be normal. Blood pressure was low as well, but not abnormal.

The aberrant heartbeats Lance warned her about were out of place at best. Their patient didn't wear a medical alert bracelet that gave witness to any serious medical conditions. A Colorado driver's license identified him as Casper English. Age thirty-four. Five foot nine. One hundred and eighty pounds.

Another nurse, Katie, pulled a photo from another of Mr. English's pockets. Her eyes locked Ashley's in terror as the red blood cells in her face scurried elsewhere, leaving her pink cheeks washed white. "It's you," she stammered.

"What?"

The young nurse held out a shaky hand. "The photo in his pocket is of you."

Ashley plucked the photo from her fingers—the image of her at her medical school graduation. Why would a stranger have this photo? She swallowed past the tension in her throat.

First things first. If I want answers, I have to save his life.

Two police officers huddled in the hall. A man found beaten in the woods certainly warranted their notification by the ER staff. His socks and shoes were missing. His shirt torn...no, sliced up the middle by something razor-sharp. A pair of worn, tattered jeans the only barrier left to protect him from the biting wind.

Why do you have my picture? The thought became intrusive. She tried to shove it away.

"What's his temperature?" Ashley asked.

"Ninety-three degrees," Lance replied.

"He has hypothermia. His heart doesn't like this low body temperature and if we don't get a handle on it, we're going to have more problems on our hands. Warm blankets. Lots of them. Let's get those IV fluids warmed up, as well."

Ashley frowned and gathered her dark brown hair into one of the ponytail holders she always kept on her wrist.

So much for getting off work on time. Lord, would it be too much to ask to have an end of shift without a major crisis?

As a favor to the night shift physician, Ashley had agreed to examine the mysterious arrival that had been dropped off by a stranger and his dog. The man who'd left him hadn't wanted to answer many questions. Ashley hadn't thought she'd walk in to find a critical patient flirting with the grim reaper.

In a flurry of activity, Lance changed out the IV tubing so the fluid ran over a warming plate. Several heated blankets were placed over their patient. Katie grabbed a set of hot lights and set them over the ER gurney, their patient like fast food waiting for delivery.

Ashley placed two fingers in the groove of the unconscious man's right wrist, finding his pulse under hers like a weak echo. His face and torso were a road map of fury to whomever Casper had run into on this bitterly cold night. Angry circular bruises of various sizes and shapes dotted his skin. Some were clearly triangular shaped, indicating an object had been used to create the injury driven into his skin at high velocity. The tip of a boot? Ashley's fingers traveled up his forearm. His skin was cold, doughy under her touch. She pulled his arm away from his torso, looking for any injuries that could be more life-threatening than the hypothermia he was suffering from.

Are you a stalker? Is that why you have my picture? And if you are, why has someone beaten you? To protect me?

Working in the ER lent credence to this question. He wouldn't be the first patient to take an unusual interest in her.

Ashley returned her attention to the unconscious man. Severely beaten was an understatement. In fact, he might find death a welcomed relief compared to the pain he would be suffering when his brain reengaged with this world. At least, Ashley hoped he would find his way back.

What little information they'd garnered from the Good Samaritan was he'd been found while he was out walking his dog in the woods. Upon discovering him, he then carried him to his truck and brought him here. It had been easier to lay him in the open bed of the pickup and he figured the short drive wouldn't do any harm. That ride likely worsened their patient's hypothermia. The story was strange and the actions of his rescuer somewhat odd, but it definitely wasn't the tallest tale Ashley had heard in her years as an ER doctor.

What was Casper doing in the woods? Alone, all by himself? Essentially left to die.

The monitor triple-beeped—its better-pay-attention-to-the-patient-because-he's-trying-to-die tone. Everyone in the room glanced at the mysterious man's heart tracing and each knew in their gut this man was starting to circle the drain.

"Start CPR. Get the defibrillator pads on him," Ashley ordered.

The ER tech and Lance turned Casper on his side and slid a CPR board underneath his back. As the tech started CPR, Lance placed two large white adhesive patches on Casper's skin.

"Charge to one-hundred-and-sixty joules," Ashley said.

Katie dialed in the electricity. The machine toned it was ready. "Everyone clear!" she yelled.

The medical staff close to the bed backed up one step. The man's body jerked slightly as the electricity coursed through his chest. Within seconds of the shock, the man's eyes bolted open and he sat straight up in bed, his brown, nearly black eyes wide with confusion. He grabbed Katie's wrist and held it firmly, his breath heaving.

Ashley's heart galloped in her chest. She'd heard stories like this, about a shock waking a patient up, but never had she seen it. She took three quick steps to the bedside and rested a gentle hand on her patient's shoulder, hoping her touch was reassuring enough to calm him down.

"Sir, you're at Castle Peak Medical Center in the emergency department. I'm Dr. Ashley Drager. You were brought here after someone found you unconscious." Ashley smoothed her hand down his arm over the tense muscles to his hand that held viselike onto the nurse. "Please, let her go. You're safe here."

The man's eyes locked her gaze. A flash of something, perhaps recognition, was gone as quickly as it came. Did he know her? Would he be able to tell her about why he had her picture? All that remained in the darkness of his irises was terror.

"Do you remember what happened to you?" Lance asked.

Ashley curled her fingers around her patient's and began to pull his appendages up one at a time. The man allowed her to do so and when the last one was released, Katie rubbed her wrist, the skin reddened from the grip.

"Do you know your name?" Ashley asked.

The man blinked at her several times and remained silent.

"Your driver's license states your name is Casper English. Is that correct?"

He began to shiver. Ashley walked to the warmer and grabbed another blanket. Her patient remained sitting, and she unfolded the worn cotton to drape over his shoulders. Just as she was about to release the linen, she saw the tattoo that branded him between his shoulder blades. The medical staff inked in black superimposed over a blazing red biohazard symbol.

Identical to the one her father had. In the same exact spot as his.

Her missing father. Gone for just over two years.

Ashley began to tremble and held the warmed blanket to her chest to drive the chill away. Her mouth gaped open, her lungs hungry for air but seemingly unable to draw breath. The room grew hazy.

"Ashley?" Lance asked.

Lance's voice brought her back to the present, and she shook her head to reengage her brain. She dropped the blanket over the man's shoulders.

What were the odds this man would possess the same unusual mark as her father?

Did this stranger hold the answer to her father's disappearance?

TWO

She had called him Casper. Dr. Ashley Drager. That was what she called herself.

The nurses were gone from the room. He huddled into the blanket she had placed over his shoulders. Never in his life could he remember being this cold. It was as if his bones were solid ice and would never stop leaching frigid water into his veins. Her hands, small, soft, yet determined, eased him back onto the raised head of the gurney.

"What's the last thing you remember?" she asked.

Her dark blue eyes seemed a safe place to be. They exerted a trusting nature, an open mind, almost a pleading for information.

The name she called him…Casper…seemed to ring true, but neither was he positive that was correct. He searched his mind for an answer to her question and all there was to draw upon was a blank well of darkness.

Casper's stomach clenched. He couldn't remember. What was the last thing he could clearly recall? What had he been doing to end up here? He pulled the blankets down that covered his chest to examine his injuries. An IV was in his left hand. He touched it lightly, the fluid running into his veins warm and soothing.

He tugged at the large patches on his chest, but Ashley grabbed his hand and pulled it down as if he were an intemperate child doing something he shouldn't. In truth, it's how he felt—young, uncertain. He honed in on her face for approval with each movement he made. Gingerly, he touched his jaw with his fingers. Several mounds of swollen flesh protruded from his skull in abnormal places, and even the slightest touch caused sharp spindles of pain to spread throughout his head. He settled against the pillow.

"I can't remember." Was this how his voice normally sounded?

Dr. Drager pulled her stethoscope from her pocket. "Let me see if I can find a reason why you're having trouble remembering. Your body temperature is very low. That could be part of it, but I'm doubtful that's the cause. You've sustained several blows to your head and that could be the answer right there, but we need to be sure you don't have any bleeding inside your skull. We're going to send some lab work and I'm going to get a CT scan of your brain." She laid the stethoscope against his chest. The normal chill he expected was warmer than his skin. "Sorry about the rude awakening. Your heart was in a lethal rhythm and the only quick way to fix that was with a little electricity."

Little?

He rested a fist in the center of his chest as counter pressure against the remnant of pain from that dose.

Clearly, there were things he did remember. He knew what things were—particularly in this room. A pen. A stethoscope. An IV. He could identify the contraption in the corner—a rapid fluid infuser. The device they'd used to get his heart rhythm normalized—a defibrillator. He knew what a doctor was. What a nurse was. He knew how to put an IV in and could easily recall other medical procedures—his fingers itching to perform them. Muscle memory existed intact. Did that mean he was in the medical field?

Casper just couldn't remember anything about himself or his circumstances. How was that possible? Was he in the medical field? Was he a nurse? A doctor? A medic? Is that why he almost felt comforted by these surroundings?

Dr. Drager reached behind her and grabbed something from the metal stand that sat next to his bed. "This is your license. At least, we assume it is. Does this help strike up a memory?"

He took the plastic ID from her hand. Scanning the details didn't jar anything loose. He shrugged and offered it back to her.

"You can keep it. We have all the information we need from it. You also had this picture with you," Dr. Drager said.

He took it from her hand and glanced at it only briefly. Someone in a graduation gown he didn't recognize. When he caught the doctor's gaze, she looked exacerbated, one eyebrow hiked higher than the other—almost as if prompting him for…what?

Must be frustrating to have a patient show up without any answers when you're trying to help them.

Reaching around, his muscles stiff and sore, he placed the items in the back pocket of his jeans. He riffled through his front pockets and withdrew a wadded piece of paper. Once he'd evened out the page—it contained an address.

"Perhaps we should give that to the police, see if it's important," Dr. Drager said.

"No!" The strength of his conviction surprised even him. She took a step back, the flash of fear quickly recov-

ered by her well-practiced, calm demeanor from han-
dling volatile patients.

*Why am I so adamant about hiding this information?
I don't even know what it means.*

"Casper—" She paused, perhaps changing her mind
about the direction she wanted to take the conversation.
"I'm trying to help you."

The blood pressure cuff squeezed his arm. "I know.
I'm very thankful."

Dr. Drager was headed out of the room when she suddenly turned on her heel and faced him. "Where did you
get your tattoo? Do you recall anything about that?"

"What tattoo?" Casper asked, the words spilling before he could search the void that was his mind.

"The one on your back. Right between your shoulder
blades. It's a medical staff superimposed on a biological
biohazard symbol." Ashley walked across the trauma
room to a box on the wall.

A sharps container.

How could he know that and not know any personal
details of his life?

"The symbol is exactly like this one." She tapped at
the box to staccato her point. There was pain in her eyes
as she looked at him. They glistened under the fluores-
cent lights.

He clenched his fists. Heat surged into his body, but
not a welcome feeling physically normalizing his body
temperature.

What he felt was anger. Unidentified. Smoldering.

And for her, he felt an ache in chest. Something akin
to sorrow.

*What's happening to me? What do these emotions
have to do with anything?*

"I feel…" He wanted to scream. Cry out. This was so maddening. "Do you know me?" he finally asked her.

She dropped her hand from the box on the wall. "I don't know you, sir."

"But we've met before…haven't we?" he asked, his heart almost begging for some sort of connection, a lifeline for his sinking psyche.

"I don't believe I've ever met you," she answered. Her eyes locked on his as if she was trying to bolster her certainty. "However, the photo you carry is of my medical school graduation. How did you get that picture?"

Her not knowing him—everything about her statement felt wrong. He felt like he knew her. That he'd been the beneficiary to personal details of her life that she was unaware of.

"Did you have a dog when you were young? A cocker spaniel? Named Lady? After the movie…" He snapped his fingers. *"Lady and the Tramp."*

Her eyes widened and then a smile placated her lips. "The tattoo on your back matches exactly to one my father has. Strangely, he's been missing for two years. You wouldn't know anything about that, would you?"

What is going on here?

Ashley nodded her head, his astonishment at her statement more an answer to her question than any words he could have spoken. "Let's get those tests done and see if we can find out why you're having trouble remembering who you are. In the meantime, we'll continue our rewarming measures. One of the nurses should be back shortly to take you to Radiology." She locked Casper's gaze. "We'll get you feeling better, Mr. English."

"Please, don't leave. We should talk."

Dr. Drager turned on her heel and left the room.

* * *

Ashley fled the trauma room, turned down the nearest vacant hall and leaned against the wall.

None of this is right. How can this patient have a picture of me? The last time I saw that photo I'd pulled it out of my father's wallet. How could this man know such a detail about my life? Was this handsome stranger plunked in my ER like some whimsical practical joke?

If so, it was elaborate. ER types were known to play pranks, but this? No, it was impossible. Too complicated.

This was too much—especially on the heels of another package being delivered to her just today. They were always accompanied by a letter, in her father's handwriting, simply requesting that she keep the items safe. One of many packages she received over the last several months.

Ashley reached into her lab coat and fingered the small envelope. It had come packaged as nondescriptly as the other ones. Addressed to her—always coming through department mail. Nothing but the simple note inside. No information on where he could possibly be. Never a return address. There were different items. Most were photos. Some with numbers on the back that didn't make any sense to her.

This time a thumb drive.

She leaned over and rested her hands on her knees hoping the light-headedness would pass. This was a known complication of the emergency department. A sight. A sound. A stranger could be the impetus of dredging up pain from the buried, murky depths of her past.

The day her father disappeared was always fresh in her mind. Few days went by without her thinking of him and those circumstances. They'd celebrated dinner together as a family. A late Christmas dinner as she'd been working. It had been her, her parents and her younger brother—to celebrate the end of her fellowship and her new job as an attending. The next morning, he was gone. Her mother said he'd slipped out for some doughnuts and coffee and just…never came home.

Nothing had ever been found of him. Not his car. No electronic fingerprints. He had to be off grid, maybe operating under a new identity. If he wasn't alive, then who was sending these packages?

To live with a ghost was worse than knowing the truth.

"Dr. Drager?"

She looked up, her vision fuzzed, and she pressed her thumb and index finger to the bridge of her nose. A headache was starting to take hold.

"Yes?" She blinked her eyes. Her vision cleared. The two officers who'd been waiting for the report on her patient stared at her expectantly.

"Any information?" one of them asked.

"Right now, he doesn't remember anything. Amnesia… likely a result of several blows to his head." She shoved her hands into her lab coat, curling her fingers around the small but bulky envelope. "Why don't you leave me your card? Give us a few hours to sort through his medical issues. Even if his CT scan is normal, I'll consult neurology for the memory loss. Until he can remember something, I don't know if you need to stay here. He can't offer any details of his attack right now."

The other officer reached into one of his coat pockets. "That would be great. We'd keep camped out, but there's been an officer-involved shooting across town. All hands on deck as they say."

Ashley took the card from the officer's hand. "Stay safe out there."

She watched them exit the department through the ambulance bay before making her way to the nerve center of the ER, the central hub where doctors and nurses mingled. She sat down at a computer and pulled up Casper's chart to enter some orders for tests when a man tapped the top of her computer screen with the tip of a cane.

Ashley flared her fingers out above her keyboard in annoyance before glancing up.

She pressed her lips together to keep from screaming.

Jared Fleming stood in front her. His bright blue eyes bored straight into her.

Her father's arch nemesis.

Who clearly didn't recognize her.

"You are?" he clipped.

He was exactly how she remembered him from her youth. Six feet, which was tall considering her five-foot-two-inch frame. Gray hair. Bushy black eyebrows.

"I asked you a question," he reiterated in the wake of her silence.

A man in a military uniform stood a few feet behind him, but Fleming was dressed in a black tailored suit. The vibrant, sapphire-blue shirt beneath it was almost too bright to look at.

"Dr...." Something in her told her not to continue. She reached up and flipped her ID badge around to cover her identity as she stood up, wishing she had a step stool so she could be eye to eye with the tyrant. "How did you get back here?"

"I don't need permission to—"

"Actually, you do need permission. Are you family of a patient?"

His eyes narrowed. "That's...complicated."

Thrusting her arm up, she pointed to the door that exited to the waiting room. "If you're not immediate family of one of our patients, then you'll have to leave."

He straightened and squared his shoulders. "I'm here

on important business. A matter of national security."
He rustled through one of his pockets. "I'm looking for
this man. Have you seen him?"

A striking photo of her patient, handsome, clean-shaven.
Unbeaten.

Casper.

She lowered her arm, her fingertips tingled.

"It's imperative that he be turned over into our care,"
Fleming said.

A sharp pain flared in her gut. The one thing she knew
about this man was that her father had told her never to
trust him. In fact, so often came this warning in the years
before he went missing that it was one of the most common memories she had of their lives together. Now, this
enemy of her missing father wanted her patient, who just
by the very nature of Jared's visit was now more firmly
connected to her father in her mind.

And if Casper disappeared like her father, then perhaps her last hope of discovering the truth would van-
ish, as well.

"If this gentleman were here, I assume you have legal
documents that say he can be relinquished into your care."

Jared narrowed his eyes. "Such paperwork will be...
forthcoming."

"Excellent. Until then, I'll need you to get off hospital property."

He rapped the bottom of his cane against her desk
like a metronome.

"Do I need to have security escort you out?" she asked,
knowing how empty a threat this was as she eyed the
seventy-year-old sentry that sat at the ER entrance pe-
rusing a newspaper.

"That won't be necessary." He tipped his head to her.
"I think I can find my way out."

Fleming motioned to his cohort. As soon as the two men disappeared through the door, Ashley sat in the chair, her head falling into her hands.

What she was contemplating was going to put her whole medical career in jeopardy.

THREE

Perhaps twenty minutes after Ashley had left him, she was back pushing a wheelchair, whisking the curtain closed over his glass doors so that he was shielded from peering eyes in the hall.

"Lance, would you mind leaving us? There's a private matter I need to discuss with our patient."

"CT just called for him," Lance said.

"Yes, exactly. You know, I'm getting off work anyway. I'll clear this matter up and then I'll take him to CT myself."

Lance looked at her blankly. "Are you...sure?"

"Absolutely." Ashley motioned her hand in front of her to try to erase his doubts. It was a rare event for a doctor to personally escort a patient to Radiology. "It's the end of your shift, too. I know you're anxious to get home to your new baby girl."

Lance's smile lit his face up. "You're right. Thanks, Ashley. It's going to take me a while to get things wrapped up and give my report. You doing this really helps."

"Have a great night," she said as he exited the room.

The interchange confused Casper. Ashley looked disheveled, out of sorts. There was a slight sheen to her forehead. A mild tremble in her shoulders. She pushed the wheelchair next to his bed, parked it and then lowered the side rails.

"We're leaving." She rounded to his left side and turned off his monitor, then began disconnecting the monitoring cables from his body.

Her words had an edge to them—her face creased with worry. The actions she took coupled with her clipped words seemed to suggest something other than a simple trip to Radiology.

"This is going to hurt," she said, taking firm fingers and ripping the defibrillation pads off his chest.

Casper gritted his teeth and suppressed a yell. Unable to keep his eyes from watering, he rubbed at the raw, burning skin.

"Sorry," she said, though she didn't sound nearly as penitent as he wanted her to be. Next, she removed the layers of clear tape that held his IV in place.

He clasped his hand over hers. "Wait, aren't they going to need this for the scan?"

She blinked at him. If he had to guess, she pondered why he would even think to ask such a question. "No, we're leaving the hospital." With a quick motion, she pulled the catheter from his arm, put a cotton ball over the site and then wrapped a piece of self-adhering dressing around his hand.

"Dr. Drager, please, what is going on?"

"Ashley... You might as well call me by my first name. I'm essentially kidnapping you."

Not that he minded, but for what reason? What had her so unnerved?

"Why are we leaving?"

She yanked one of the blankets from his chest, settled it in the wheelchair and then eased his legs so his feet were resting against the floor. The room spun.

"Sit here for a minute. You're probably dizzy from lay-ing down for so long. If you fall I won't be able to pick you up by myself and I can't call for help."

Casper pressed two fingers into his temple until the sensation passed. "If I'm going to allow myself to be kid-napped then I need to know why."

"Does the name Jared Fleming mean anything to you?"

Nothing registered. He shook his head.

"Something very weird is going on here. You show up, amnestic—almost beaten to death. Your tattoo is the same exact one my father, who's been missing, has. You arrive with a photo of me in your pocket. And just as I was trying to insanely, and with a lot of denial I might add, talk myself out of thinking that you having a con-nection to me and my father was utter lunacy, my father's arch nemesis shows up asking me to relinquish you into his custody without any legal documentation support-ing such an action."

Every last ounce of strength that Casper possessed, which was precious little at this point in time, melted away like the snow under a newly bright Colorado sun. Trouble was, he wanted to assist her, but doubted he could lift a finger to even help himself. Ashley had every right to make such assumptions and clearly she was operating for his benefit, albeit through selfish needs of her own.

Can I blame her? I'd do exactly the same thing under these circumstances. Sticking with her might provide the answers that I need. Maybe she's the key to getting my memory back.

Casper inhaled sharply and gathered up the last ves-tiges of his energy. He eased himself up and pivoted into the wheelchair. Now all he wanted to do was go to bed and sleep the rest of this day away. She tucked the blanket around his torso.

"If we get out of here, what exactly is your plan?" Casper asked.

Ashley bent over and unlocked his wheelchair, her exhalation whispering past his ear. A hint of citrusy body spray lingered in her wake.

"I haven't thought that far ahead. I'll probably take you to my mother's house. If you knew my father maybe she knows you and can help me figure out if I should be worried about Jared coming for you or not."

"So you don't necessarily believe your father? That this man is his enemy?"

"It's hard to put faith and trust in a man who deserted his family. My father said a lot of crazy things. Did a lot of scary stuff, but the one thing he was always consistent about for several years before he disappeared was his hatred of the man who just came looking for you."

Ashley wheeled him to the door and peeked around the curtain. Seemingly satisfied, she yanked the curtain aside and pushed him through the sliding glass door. Making two quick turns, they came to a vacant hall. She locked the chair.

"Hopefully, everyone will be tied up for shift report. I need to grab my coat and purse. Don't go anywhere."

She disappeared behind the door to the doctor's lounge and he was left alone. The chill was beginning to dissipate and he appreciated the warmth the blanket provided. If he'd been found in the snow, it likely hadn't melted in the few hours since his arrival, particularly with the blackness of night making its claim against the last remnants of daylight.

Just as the door clicked closed behind Ashley, Lance rounded the corner.

"Mr. English, are you lost?"

The spry nurse rounded to the back of his wheelchair and unlocked the brake. "CT is wondering where their patient is."

Casper took his left hand and shoved the brake into place just as Ashley came through the door, zipping up her coat and holding her purse and a large manila envelope.

"It's okay, Lance. I've got it. Just didn't want to come back to the department after I dropped him off."

Lance nodded, though unsurely, but backed away so she could scoot behind the chair.

After a few more turns through the halls of the ER, Ashley came to a side entrance. "My car's not far, but it's going to be hard to get this wheelchair through the lot with all the snow."

He nodded and flipped the footrests up. He stood, shakily. Ashley scooted next to him and fit herself under his right arm. Just the right size to act as a crutch. He leaned heavily against her, worried that she might topple over, but her strength surprised him and they soldiered through the door into the biting wind.

They walked perhaps thirty steps until they reached a pine-green Toyota Highlander. She pressed her key fob twice, unlocking the passenger door, and he poured into the seat, barely able to hold himself upright. After she grabbed the blanket and hastily threw it over his chest, she buckled the seat belt around him and hurried to the driver's side. After starting the car, she turned on the heat, and he was immediately met with a blast of cold air that the thinly threaded blanket did little to protect him against, and the chill reasserted itself with a vengeance. His teeth chattered.

She turned down the flow and put the SUV in Reverse, making her way through the parking lot.

Just as the parking lot arm was about to release them, a security guard came running toward their vehicle from the left.

"We shouldn't stay," Casper warned.

Ashley powered down her window, ignoring Casper. "Everything okay, Noah?"

"Dr. Drager. A patient has been reported missing from the hospital. A Casper English."

She glanced back at Casper and he shrugged, his mind a muddled mess of frozen brain cells.

"He's all right," Ashley called out the window. "Mr. English is here with me, and he's refused any further medical care. He's asked me to drive him home."

"Dr. Drager, as you know, it would be highly unusual—even against policy—for you to transport a patient off hospital property regardless of their wishes."

"It's fine, Noah. He's an old friend. I think the hospital will—"

Ashley jerked back and Casper felt the warm spray of something hit his face. When he looked left, he saw a fine mist of red droplets covering Ashley's hands, which gripped the steering wheel so tightly they were stark white. Noah staggered back a few steps away from the car, a hand held tightly against his neck as blood gushed between his fingers. The guard dropped to his knees.

"Drive!" Casper yelled.

Ashley reached for the car's door handle. "I can't leave him," she cried.

The next shot cracked the back driver's-side passenger window.

"Ashley, go! We're going to die if we stay here."

The next shot punctured through Ashley's open window into the dashboard.

Ashley stepped on the gas and flew out of the parking lot.

* * *

The night rushed past Ashley. Light snow flurries danced unabashed. Everything seemed quiet and peaceful other than the fact that she was speeding through neighborhoods preparing for slumber—braking, sliding on the icy streets. The dropping temperature crystallized what little snow had melted during the day. Ashley used a wet wipe from her glove box to clean the blood spray off her hands. She took another and wiped the left side of her face.

She was crying. Thinking of Noah. She prayed her call to the emergency department and 911 about Noah's injury and the shots fired got help to Noah in time and no one else was hurt. When one of her fellow physicians pressed her for information, she'd disconnected the call.

Ashley's thoughts spun. Adrenaline-fueled blood rushed through her head and there was a faint pitched whine ringing in her ears that masked Casper's voice. She looked at him, barely able to see through her tears, wondering if she'd have to resort to reading lips because she couldn't discern what his words conveyed. Gibberish. What she did see was the surprise and apprehension that covered his face.

It was the worry that concerned her the most. Who were these people?

This is exactly why patients can't talk when I tell them bad news. Why they can't process any information. What is this insanity?

Clenching her teeth, she wiped the tears from her face.

I have to pull myself together. Crying isn't going to help either one of us right now.

She gripped the steering wheel so hard her hands ached. Casper glanced behind them, his movements stilted. "They're coming." A simple statement filled with so much danger.

Ashley glanced up in her rearview mirror. A black SUV was quickly closing the distance. Perhaps two blocks behind. A crack of metal jolted the car.

A gunshot punctured her tailgate. Ashley pressed her foot into the accelerator.

Casper narrowed his eyes. "Nearest highway?"

Ashley tried to think. First thing, she needed to shake them off their tail. She whipped the steering wheel right—so tight was the turn that the car lifted up briefly on two wheels. Ashley's heart climbed into her throat.

After a series of three Z-turns, their pursuers remained right on their tail.

"That's not going to work. They're more experienced at this than you," Casper said.

"Who is 'they'?" Ashley yelled, briefly glancing Casper's way. Her hands were slick with sweat.

"Get to the highway."

Fine. What sense did it make to let the confused, amnesiac patient determine their course of action? Not much, but there hadn't been a med school class on outrunning thugs who intended to kill innocent people, so she gave him this one suggestion.

Two more turns and Ashley sped up the entrance ramp onto the highway. She merged quickly into traffic.

"Fast lane," Casper said.

No, that wasn't going to work. If driving was their skill, these delinquents would simply follow them until she ran out of gas. Somehow, she had to shake them.

There was a semi in the slow lane. Ashley began to position herself next to it...slowing their vehicle down.

"What are you doing?" Casper asked.

The black SUV sidled up next to them. The windows

were tinted so dark she couldn't discern the shape of any of the men inside.

The window of the SUV cracked open. Ashley hedged up until she and the semi were nose to nose. There was perhaps half a mile to the next exit.

Quickly, she looked left. The tip of a gun showed through the small gap in the window. The back passenger window on Casper's side shattered. Air waffled noisily through the car so hard that her eardrums ached with the pressure. Ashley veered right. Casper turned his head her way reflexively, his head hunched down, expecting to impact against the tractor trailer's side.

"Whatever you're going to do, do it now!" Casper yelled.

Ashley stomped on the accelerator, pulling ahead of the semi, and at the last possible moment jerked the steering wheel hard right, careening in front of the sixteen-wheeler and onto the exit ramp.

In her wake, she heard the blare of the truck's horn in complaint. Ashley shook so badly she could hardly grip the steering wheel. Her legs quivered.

Casper laid a reassuring hand over hers. "Nice job."

His touch had a surprising calming effect. Her father hadn't been the touchy-feely type. She could count the number of hugs she'd received from him growing up on one hand. One of her regrets after her father disappeared was not having had a closer relationship with him.

Ashley made several more turns, attempting to put a confusing amount of distance between them and their attackers.

Casper pointed at the twenty-four hour grocery store coming up on their right. Perhaps thirty minutes had passed without evidence of them being followed. He motioned his finger up and down. "Turn in here. Park close to the front."

Ashley's body felt like a tangle of nerves on fire. "Shouldn't we keep moving?"

One of Casper's hands gripped the dashboard. He looked as lost as he no doubt felt. This wasn't good in any measure. They were being hunted. This was something both of them understood. How could an amnesiac man and a healer ward off armed gunmen?

Since Ashley's mind remained a muddled mess and she couldn't think of any alternative argument, she did as Casper asked and parked her car among the other vehicles, but not directly under a parking light, hoping the darkness would offer some disguise. She turned the car off and killed the lights and looked at the world in front of her.

It was that peaceful seasonal lull. Just after the holidays but before all the outdoor lights were taken down. The hubbub of the holidays was over and the spirit of Christmas could be enjoyed without the accompanying stress.

Casper scanned the road that ran past the grocery store. He was sitting up and forward in his seat, a guard dog on alert. His continuously roving eyes narrowed and Ashley's chest ached as she held her breath.

A black SUV was turning into the lot. How was it possible for them to be found so quickly? Her mouth dried. Did they duck down? Get out? Stay as still as statues?

Ashley looked for some direction from Casper, but he remained pensive and silent next to her. They both watched the vehicle turn into the lot and park a few rows away, and then a mother with two teen daughters emerged.

"We need a different car," Casper said.

"As in steal one?"

"Unless you have another spare vehicle that's perhaps not registered to you or anyone you know. What I know is that this Jared Fleming is going to know who you are now. It looks like he has some resources at his disposal that maybe fly under the letter of the law. We need to disappear."

Her mouth gaped open. Casper was serious.

Is that what her father had done? Gone into hiding because of Jared?

Ashley shook her head. "What do we do after that? Where do we go? I don't think going to my mother's is a good idea anymore. We don't know who these men are or what they want. I won't put her life in danger."

"Well, we do know what they want…at least partially."

He was right. "They want you, but why?"

Casper shrugged. "And is it connected to your father? I'm not one to believe in coincidences. I don't know the meaning behind these events and I don't know why I was attacked or by whom, but I think we're together for a reason and that's been orchestrated."

By God. Those were the two words he didn't end with but meant wholeheartedly. That was what she felt like he was saying to her. Her view on God? That He was a disconnected, distant being that cared little for the everyday affairs of humans. Just like her father was currently and had been from her earliest memories. It's not that she didn't believe in God, it's just that she didn't think He orchestrated the minutiae of her life.

Thoughts tousled through her mind, looking for a way to connect with one another. Was the thumb drive she'd received important to the events that just happened? Should she tell Casper about it? What did she know about this drifter sitting next to her? Her father might be missing for nefarious reasons. Nothing said that her father wasn't involved in some criminal undertaking. Who was to say that he and Casper weren't part of some criminal underbelly and she'd just tethered herself to him from one assumption—that her father had told her never to trust Jared Fleming and that man had wanted her patient.

But could she trust her father?

Ashley shook the thoughts away. She'd keep the thumb drive a secret…for now. She needed more data to make an informed decision.

Casper wanting to steal a car boiled down to her doing it. What condition was he in to go searching through a bustling parking lot looking for a vehicle to abscond? Breaking the law could lead to repercussions by the Board of Healing Arts. She could lose her medical license. What was stopping her from just calling the police? Wouldn't that be a wiser choice?

Her instincts told her not to. What help had the police been to her and her family after her father's disappearance? Not a scrap of evidence, a lead or hint that he was even still alive had been given to them from law enforcement. The packages were the only evidence she clung to, but receiving them didn't mean he was alive. The first sense of promise that she might discover answers was from this stranger who possessed the same unusual tattoo and had landed in her ER as if gifted from desperation.

Her heart sank. Her cell phone…was it already being traced? Probably. Or was she being paranoid? Probably not. She pulled the device from her back pocket, but before she could power it down, maybe even destroy it, she had to do one thing.

Mom, I'm okay. You may not hear from me for a while. I love you. Please, don't worry.

Immediately after the message showed delivered she turned the phone off. Casper nodded approvingly. Weird thing was, his assent meant something to her. An alliance, though tenuous, was forming.

Was turning the phone off enough? Could they trace it powered down? She didn't have any experience in evading the law—or the lawless. Casper unlocked his seat belt and began sifting through his pockets and removed the wadded piece of paper.

"We need to go here," he said, pointing to the slip that held the penned address.

"How can you be sure?"

"I'm not, but I don't know what else to do."

"Do you know exactly where it is?"

"In Colorado. We'll need a map. You can buy one in there."

"No credit cards I'm assuming."

"Right."

Ashley reached for her seat belt. Her heart pounded against her moral conviction of what he'd asked her to do. Did she not have a say? In fact, there could be an easy argument that she was of sounder mind and body than he was.

"I'm not doing what you ask." Ashley turned and faced him. "I can't steal a car. Whatever is happening here, I've already done enough to put my medical career at risk. Taking a patient from the hospital, if you corroborate my story that you came willingly…"

"You didn't take me from the hospital without my permission," Casper said. "That's not a lie. I could have stopped you."

She raised an eyebrow at the unlikeliness of that statement. Truly, he was in little condition to stop her from doing much. "Then that charge I can survive. The hospital won't be happy that I drove a patient home, but a slap on the wrist might be punishment enough in their eyes."

"I sense a rebuttal coming."

"I just won't steal a car. I'm willing to go on this… adventure with you to a certain point, but I can't break the law."

"Fine. I understand. This is all very confusing to me, as well—"

"I can only imagine."

"Then what is your plan?"

She reached behind her, grabbed her purse and reached into its depths for her wallet. She opened it up and pushed her finger into the gap, a place she opened in the lining, for one of the last things her father ever gave her.

"My dad told me that if I was ever in trouble—'weird trouble' was the phrase he used, then I was to call this person and ask for help." She opened the paper and traced her father's blocky penmanship. "Horace Longbottom."

She jolted as Casper laughed. "Seriously?"

In fact, he laughed so hard, he had to use the corners of the blanket to dab the tears from his eyes.

Heat flushed Ashley's face. "Like you have room to laugh at a name… Casper? As in the friendly ghost? What sane parent names their kid something they know will be an automatic reason to bully their child?"

Casper raised his hand at her as his laughter died. "Point taken. I'm sorry. It's just…sometimes you need to laugh when things get dark."

True. That was one thing she could agree with. Black humor was a mechanism she used in the ER all the time to get through hectic shifts. It was a salve she and her coworkers depended on.

"You're forgiven." She opened her wallet again. Only about seventy-five dollars in cash. Enough to make a phone call, and buy some items for Casper. He was still shivering intermittently beside her. A slight wintery breeze drifted through the shot-out windows. Something hot to drink would help while they waited. "Stay here," she instructed.

Ashley stepped from the vehicle and began to walk into the store, wondering if she'd be shot on sight just like her friend Noah.

FOUR

Casper watched Ashley walk away. The intensifying swirling snow obstructed his vision of her as she neared the entrance to the grocery store.

Will this be the last time I see her? Is she truly calling for help or surrendering herself? Is this drive to figure out what happened to her father enough to bring her back to me?

Lord, I don't know what's happening here, but I know You're always with me, a light on my dark path. Show me what I'm supposed to do here? Give me back my memories, please. I don't want this woman to be hurt by whatever it is I'm involved in.

In the short time he and Ashley had been together, she'd definitely made a mark on his psyche. There was a lingering presence of her in his memories—he was sure of it. She was strikingly beautiful. Dark brunette hair with fiery red highlights echoed the tenacious spirit within her. He eyed his left hand. No ring there, but it could have been taken during his attack. Casper rejected the thought. He brought his forearms up into the moonlight—a full moon, now bright, looked pregnant with mischievousness. His skin was tan and there lacked the characteristic white mark on his ring finger that would be there if an item of jewelry like that had been taken. Even without the ostentatious clue, he felt like he was alone…single. Not connected with anyone. A free spirit as they say.

That feeling left something hollow within him. Like he'd been alone too long and yearned for that to change. Was this true or just the frustrated musings of a man who only had faint shadows of an impression of himself and little else?

The snow seemingly parted as she walked back to the SUV holding a carrier of steaming drinks in her hand with a plastic grocery bag in the other. Casper reached across and cracked open the door and she hopped back into the driver's seat. People glanced at the shattered windows as they walked by. Hopefully, their curiosity would be self-limiting.

"Horace should be here in about fifteen minutes. He said to look for a red tow truck. I told him about where we were parked and the model of my car. He said he doesn't want us walking out in the open and was a little upset at our choice of stopping places." She raised one eyebrow at Casper as if exerting her objections over his plan was something he should have considered more seriously. "He definitely wanted to meet somewhere more secluded, but didn't think it wise to get back on the roads."

Ashley handed him a sweatshirt and he begrudgingly put it on—obviously a deeply discounted Christmas item.

"Sorry, I couldn't find any shoes I thought would fit your feet."

Casper turned the key in the ignition to the point where the radio could turn on and scanned through the

AM channels to see if there was any sort of alert out with their description. Thus far, they seemingly hadn't been followed and there also wasn't an increase in police activity that he noticed. Then again, they had traveled quite a distance from the hospital.

Lack of law enforcement could be both good and bad. If the local police were involved, then whoever was looking for him didn't seem to mind someone knowing about it. On the downside, if local law enforcement wasn't involved then the people who came for him were part of the underbelly of society. Criminals didn't involve the police in their endeavors.

Darkness meant secrets. Secrets usually meant danger.

"You need to drink something warm to help with the hypothermia. I didn't know what you'd like so I got one of everything." She pointed to each drink as she named them. "Coffee, chai, black tea and hot chocolate."

He smiled. It was disheartening and charming in the same breath. He wished she hadn't spent what cash she had on hand on something so frivolous, but the deep-seated cold that had taken residence in his body cried for something…anything…to increase his body temperature, and he didn't think asking her to snuggle was an option.

"Thank you," he said. Most people drank coffee so why not try that first? He slurped at the liquid and his taste buds cried out in horror, and it was all he could do not to spit the brine out onto Ashley's lap. He clenched his eyes and swallowed. "No, not this. It's terrible," he said and she took the cup from his hands.

"It's all right. I'm not much of a coffee fan, either."

"Well, what do you like?" Casper asked. Perhaps they had the same taste.

"Any of the other three. I've got cream and sugar in my pocket for the tea if you taste it and don't like it plain."

"How about the hot chocolate?" he said, taking the cup from the cardboard tray. He didn't miss the slight down-turn of her lips at his choice. "Tea, then."

She pushed gently at his hands to keep him from putting the cup back. "No, it's all right. I'll take the chai. Close enough to hot chocolate anyway."

He sipped the liquid. "Peppermint?"

She nodded. "One of the few things I like about the holidays."

Casper let the liquid slosh playfully over his tongue. A brief vision sparked in his mind. His younger self perhaps. A man and woman. Another male child. Brother, maybe? A train circling the bottom of a Christmas tree.

Ashley held the cup with chai between her hands. "Did you remember something?"

Casper shrugged. How could he know what was real and what wasn't when he didn't have a sense of his true self?

"The littlest things can make you recall memories. A taste. A smell. Sometimes those impressions can be even more powerful than pictures."

"Why one of the few things?" Casper asked.

Ashley's eyes widened. "What?"

"You said there were *few* things that you liked about the holidays. Why is that?"

"It was just after Christmas that my father disappeared. We'd had a late Christmas dinner together. The next morning, he goes out for pastries and just never came home. No trace of him has ever been found."

"Do you have a picture of your father?"

Ashley pulled her wallet out again. "No laughing. The

last family photo we had taken was when I graduated from college."

She pulled it out. A classic studio photo. Her mother and father sitting on a bench with Ashley and her brother standing behind them. Casper traced the man's face with his thumb. Almost a feeling of kinship, but his mind remained blank.

The drone of an engine sounded behind them. Ashley tapped at his leg. "It's him. Horace."

Casper pulled the blanket tightly around him. He looked out the window. No passersby at the moment. How ridiculous would he look walking in a parking lot dressed in ripped jeans, no shoes or socks, and a discounted sweatshirt featuring Santa and Rudolph high-fiving each other?

Ashley had already exited the vehicle and he quickly followed suit. She opened the passenger door on the tow truck, scooted over to the middle and motioned Casper inside.

Standing on the running board, Casper hoisted himself up and sat down on the torn leather seat. One jagged-edged spring poked his thigh from a particularly thin spot. He reached over to shake Horace's hand. His hair was dark red, bordering on brown, and cinched tightly with a rubber band at the base of his neck. A lighter red beard, scraggly and unkempt. The inner border of his hairline and the upper portion of his beard were tinged with gray, giving the appearance of a silver, not gold, halo that might have sank forward, sticking to the outer reaches of his face. Blue eyes that held both secrets and a smile engaged Casper's. From the gap between his teeth he juggled two toothpicks, the space serving as an anchor point.

"Better get movin'," Horace said, as he glanced in his rearview mirror.

That was when Casper saw a vehicle slowly driving down each parking lot row.

Clearly looking for someone.

From the outside, Horace's garage looked how you'd expect a tow truck business to look. The inside was a different story. Behind a few doors, down a hidden flight of stairs, and it was like she and Casper had entered another world. The only word Ashley could use to describe the room was *bunker*, as in fully prepped for most things shy of an apocalyptic event.

It held two twin beds with a small bathroom off to the side. Ashley could see Casper eyeing the mattress wistfully and couldn't imagine how tired he felt. Beaten. Hypothermic. He needed rest.

"Is it okay if Casper sleeps?" Ashley asked Horace.

"This is both a place to rest…and hide." He shifted his gaze to Casper. "Looks like you could use a few hours."

Casper shifted uncomfortably on his feet. It was as if he didn't know the right decision to make. Considering what he'd been through, indecisiveness could be a natural symptom of head injury and hypothermia. His brain cell connections had been interrupted and then frozen. The neurons were trying to find their way back to one another. Sleep was an excellent treatment—the only way to get the mind to rest and heal.

"You should nap," Ashley said to Casper, and was mildly surprised he didn't fight her on the issue and immediately lay down. She stepped to the other bed and grabbed a few of the quilts at the base and unfolded them over his body—his eyelids already closing.

Medically, she worried about an undiagnosed brain injury. Was he bleeding inside? Would his closed eyes remain that way? Years of medicine had been practiced without the diagnostic tests as readily available as they were today. Ashley realized how much she would need to rely on her medical training.

Did I make the right decision taking him from the hospital? Have I risked his life by not having the information those medical tests would have provided?

Horace motioned her into the next room, which held a mixture of computer equipment. The place was tidy. Not a smudge of grease marred the surfaces of the myriad of tables crammed into the space. He pulled out a chair and Ashley sat down.

"Thank you," she said. "I never dreamed I'd have to use your number. Sometimes I couldn't tell if the things my father told me were true or not."

"Probably a mixture. It's hard…this game he's playing," Horace said, turning away from her, seemingly not wanting to elaborate on his point.

"How do you know my father?" Ashley asked. Perhaps reminiscing with Horace would enable her to learn some of her father's secrets.

"We met in the years following the Gulf War in Iraq. Guess it was early '90s. Seems like two lifetimes ago." Horace shrugged, his eyes locked on something behind her.

Ashley turned around and saw the wall of military photos. She narrowed her eyes to see if she could make her father out. She knew so little of his past. "What were the two of you doing there?"

"I was serving in the military. I was part of a small peacekeeping force left behind to stabilize the country.

Your father was with the United Nations Special Commission at the time investigating the claim that Iraq had a biological weapons program."

Ashley's throat tightened. "You're serious?"

"It doesn't surprise me that he didn't share much of this with you. When you're on foreign lands, you never know who will turn out to be friend or foe."

"Lands?"

"Excuse me?"

"As in plural," Ashley said. "Like Iraq wasn't the only foreign country he'd been in."

Horace drummed his fingers. "You're smart, just like he was."

Ashley didn't know how to take his comment. Was he being condescending? Just making a factual observation? Her mother's advice came to her. First, assume people are operating with good intentions at heart. After all, Horace had picked them up from a pretty dicey situation with no questions asked and it looked like he was used to helping other people in similar predicaments.

"Did they find bioweapons?" Ashley asked.

Horace nodded. "Did you know it's been illegal since 1972 to manufacture bioweapons? There's an international treaty in place." Horace raked his fingers through his patchy red-and-gray beard. "Your father shared a story with me once about watching footage of a government's chemical weapons attack against its own citizens. It horrified him. He said he watched women running, carrying children, fleeing from the city, and then they just dropped...dead."

Ashley swallowed hard. She'd heard of events like this in the Middle East. For her own sanity, she didn't watch the footage of such carnage. Sometimes, it was hard to relate to something thousands of miles away, but her father had witnessed these horrors. What did that do to a person?

"That scene of that mother and daughter broke him. He'd just found out that your mother was pregnant with you and it became a mission of his to stop these attacks from happening wherever he could. However, he'd specialized in medicine—not chemistry. He found biological agents fascinating. That's where he decided to concentrate his work."

"What did he find in Iraq?"

"There was evidence of anthrax and a few other agents."

"Do you know what happened to my father? Where he's been these last two years?"

Horace's face twitched as if his body was betraying his mental conflict. It was clear to Ashley that he knew something, but why should they trust one another?

Ashley tried a different approach. "Are you helping him?"

"I always help…but I try to avoid a lot of direct person-to-person contact. For you, because of Russell, I've made an exception. Meeting with fugitives can be dangerous. I don't want others to discover what I have here."

"How do you help?"

"Sometimes people need to disappear. That's what I help with."

"Did you do the same for my father?" Ashley asked.

Horace offered a slight smile. "You're crafty. Asking the same question a different way will still not get me to answer."

Some said intuition was built on years of experience and perhaps Ashley had those years whether or not the stories her father shared with her were true. Something felt kind and honest about Horace. Ashley reached into the pocket of her lab coat, which held the thumb drive she'd been sent with the unsigned note admonishing her to *keep it safe*.

She opened her palm and revealed it to Horace. His eyes widened briefly, but then settled. He tried to assume a nonplussed manner.

"I think my father sent this to me."

"He did and I…helped…get the packages to you," Horace said.

Horace reached out, Ashley assumed to take the drive from her for examination, maybe even put it in one of his computers to see the information that it contained. Instead, he closed her fingers back over it.

"You don't want to see what's on it?"

Horace shook his head. "For your father to ask me for help means he's in desperate straits."

"What makes you say that?"

"Because you're his daughter and the last thing he'd do would be to send you something that would put your life in danger."

Ashley's nerves tingled. She felt light-headed. Was this the very thing that had caused Noah to get shot? Was this specifically what Fleming was looking for?

Horace eyed her and smoothed his tongue on the inside of his cheek. "He likely sent this to you because he doesn't know who he can trust within the organization he's currently employed by."

"Which is?"

He laughed, gently, as if her question was one of the most amusing things he'd heard in a while. "What I can say is that your father has a plan. Just follow the clues."

Ashley blinked twice…her mind stalled on the comment.

This is what her mother said often, only she didn't mean her missing father—she meant the God she believed in. God was involved on a personal level—as much as He'd be allowed to be. Ashley tossed the thought aside. This wasn't a path she wanted to go down. A philosophical discussion about God's plan for her life.

"There were pictures in some of them. I should get them so you can see—"

"Ashley," Horace said, his voice raised. "I'm happy to help get you and Casper what you need and help with other types of information. I'm an open book about anything that you see here, but your father is the keeper of many secrets...terrible secrets. Things about the current state of our civilization that you'd pray would never come true, but in fact have been experienced by millions of people the world over."

"Like that mother and the daughter," Ashley said, a coldness spreading through her.

"Exactly. I had to leave that darkness behind. To dwell on it became too much for me. It wasn't healthy. It wasn't a battle that I wanted to fight. Your father...I know he's saved lives, but the secrets he carries—if they're exposed—people are not going to be happy about it."

Ashley's throat tightened. She found it difficult to take a deep breath. Exactly what had she gotten involved with by taking Casper from the hospital? Or was it the other way around? Had she put Casper in more danger with her actions? She dismissed the thought. Each of them seemingly had pieces of this puzzle that if reconstructed would likely reveal what had happened to her father. Horace didn't seem to give any indication that he was no longer alive.

Only problem was, one of them couldn't remember

where his puzzle pieces were, and so joining together these random packages she'd received over the last six months and the clues they held was like trying to construct a puzzle without the picture on the box.

Which felt impossible.

FIVE

Casper felt a light hand on his shoulder shaking him gently. Was there an inch left of his body that didn't ache? Silently, he hoped that if he ignored the sensation long enough, the person would just go away. His mind begged him to stay asleep.

"Casper. Wake up."

Her voice. Ashley's voice. It was warm, gentle and soothing. The only sound tempting enough to draw his eyes open despite the pain he felt. He opened one eye first. The light in the room intensified his headache. Ashley, realizing he was having trouble with the brightness of the room, quickly clicked off the small bedside lamp that sat on a nightstand between the two beds.

"What time is it?" Casper asked.

"It's just after midnight. You've been sleeping for about three hours."

Casper tried to get up, but winced in pain. Ashley was sitting next to his bed in a rickety metal folding chair. She reached behind her and Horace handed her a glass of water and some pills.

"I want you to take these," Ashley stated.

"What are they? I don't like to take medicine." He said

it with such assurance he wondered if that was a little of his true nature coming through.

"It's just an over-the-counter pain reliever. You must have a splitting headache."

He did in fact. Casper eased up onto his elbows, but was immediately overtaken by dizziness. He leaned his head against the wall until the sensation passed. When he opened his eyes, the room wasn't spinning like a gyroscope anymore. He scooted up until he could rest his upper body against the wall. Ashley held out her hand. Her fingers brushing against his was unexpectedly comforting. He palmed the pills into his mouth and washed them down with half a glass of water.

Horace pulled up another chair and presented two plates of food—a simple offering of fruit, cheese and crackers.

"How do you feel otherwise?" Ashley asked.

Casper took stock of his body. His chest had some mild areas of soreness. With timid, gentle fingers he pressed the bones of his face. Definitely sore. Sometimes, his brain felt off-kilter inside his skull, as if it would intermittently break free of its moorings and induce the feeling he used to enjoy in his youth after a merry-go-round ride.

Except this wasn't nearly as enjoyable.

How can I remember something so easily from my childhood, but not remember much of my adult life? What is the last thing I remember? How do I feel? Physically spent. Mind gone. If I'm supposed to be keeping Ashley safe, I'm failing miserably in every aspect.

Her voice splintered his thoughts. "Don't try too hard to remember." She placed the plate of food on his lap. "I want you to eat something. Let's see how your stomach can handle it."

Casper took two apple wedges and a slice of cheddar cheese, making an apple-cheddar sandwich, and he quickly took a bite before his queasy stomach revolted. Soon he'd find out if the unsettled feeling in his gut was hunger or not.

As he started to make another sandwich, he noticed Ashley's eyes opened widely. "Something wrong?" Casper asked.

"It's just that...my father used to do the same thing. I've just never seen anyone else eat apples and cheese together like that—using apples like crackers."

Casper shrugged. Was it all that unusual? Maybe.

Horace pulled a group of pictures from a worn manila envelope. "You two might be interested in looking at these photos. I thought I'd met Casper before, if only briefly. Maybe they could spark a memory or two."

Casper watched as Ashley leafed through them. "They look like they were taken in a jungle. Doesn't look like anywhere in the US."

"No, definitely not in the US," Horace agreed.

Ashley flipped the photo in Casper's direction. "It's you...and my father."

Casper set his plate of food next to him and took the photo from Ashley's fingers. She was right. It did seem to be in the jungle. Heavy vines. A few monkeys in the foreground. Where could this have been?

"What's your father's name?" Casper asked.

"Russell Drager," Ashley said.

There was some familiarity with the name. Russell had his arm around Casper's shoulders like a father would pose with a son. He closed his eyes and tried to remember something of his own family. Yes, he had parents. A sibling? That seemed fuzzier...vacant.

Focus on what's in front of you.

Clearly he was chummy with Ashley's old man.

He handed the photo back to Horace. "Do the other photos help give any indication of where these might have been taken?"

Ashley shook her head. "Nothing that I can see. My father didn't share much with me about his travels. I'm not even sure my mother knows the extent of them."

Something seemed amiss to Casper. He directed his gaze to Horace. "Why do you have these?"

Horace pressed his lips together. "I took these pictures."

Ashley's eyes widened. "Where were they taken?"

"In Liberia."

"Explains the jungle feel of the photos," Casper said. "When were they taken?"

"During the 2014 Ebola outbreak," Horace verified.

"What were we doing there?" Casper asked.

"What Russell does best—hunting down secret biological weapons."

"In Liberia?" Casper asked. "I've never heard that there was a concern about such a program in that part of the world."

"Just because a country doesn't have its own weapons program doesn't mean they can't provide...let's say... specimens for the cause. Sometimes they don't even know foreign entities are on their land trying to find them."

Casper motioned to look at the photo again. "Did you know me at the time? Do you know why I was there?" Casper asked Horace.

"He merely called you his assistant. I wasn't there but maybe two days."

"Why were you there, Horace? Seems a little far afield from the work you do here," Ashley said.

"I aided in the transportation of specimens back to the US for testing." He pointed to Casper. "You and Russell were trying to find someone who was known to hunt mutated viruses and sell them to those practicing outside the law. When the Soviet Union collapsed, there were many scientists who were barely eking out an existence in their own country. They were paid a pittance for highly specialized work. After that event, many found that they could make a lot more money selling their knowledge to foreign entities. Sometimes, you can track a man by the things he creates. Their weapons will have a particular DNA signature. The two of you were working to catalog information on that Ebola strain, if needed, for future reference."

"But you won't tell us exactly who Russell and I were working for?" Casper asked.

"That's not for me to say."

Ashley handed the group of photos back to Horace. "It was worth a try. I'm just sad they didn't jog his memory."

Casper's heart caved a little. He hated being this ineffective. Why couldn't he remember what he was doing with Ashley's father in Liberia? Had it simply been a bug-hunting mission? Or had they been looking for a person? And if he and Russell had worked together, then who had they worked for?

"What I can tell you is this," Horace said. "These men who are after you mean business. If they catch you, I don't think you'd come out of it alive. Not on your own."

Casper swallowed hard. Were the two of them together merely walking to their own deaths?

If they were, was there anything Casper could do to stop it?

After sleeping a few hours, Ashley and Casper were on the road again. Horace had provided them an old clunker of a car. He said the older the better; it had to be before 2010 because then the car wouldn't be equipped with GPS tracking. He said for the time being, it was best to put Ashley's car on a semi headed the opposite direction. If she wanted, she could contact him at some point in the future to get it back.

They were phoneless, which also meant she couldn't rely on GPS programs to help her find the address in Casper's pocket. Horace had printed out several maps and a computer-generated list of directions.

In some respects, this area seemed familiar to her, as if she'd traveled these roads at one time or another in her life. It felt free in a sense, not to be tied to technology. She couldn't imagine who was trying to find her right now. Her thoughts drifted back to Noah. Was the hospital trying to find her to make sure she was okay? Or were the police trying to find her to question her about taking a patient from the hospital? Sure, security footage revealed she was the driving force behind Casper's elopement. Did law enforcement want to ask her about Casper? About Noah?

Was her mother okay? Her brother?

If anything bothered her more than these questions it was worrying about her mother. Ashley knew if her mother couldn't get ahold of her she'd be convinced she'd suffered a mishap like her father had.

The sun was up. It was late morning. She'd been driving since dawn. She glanced to her right, where Casper slept in the passenger's seat. They were hours away from this address. They were headed deep into the mountains. Why not let him slumber? Ashley's medical training had prepared her for long hours with little rest. At some point that gave diminishing returns, but she was okay for now—for the day. After that, she'd need to sleep.

Horace had traded Casper's Christmas sweatshirt for a pair of ill-fitting jeans, a flannel shirt, socks and boots. He looked comfortable. She didn't know how it was possible to look so peaceful with his injured head bouncing against the window with every bubble she hit in the road. She continued to worry that taking him from the hospital before completing a CT scan had been a bad idea.

Ashley struck the thought from her mind. If he'd had a serious brain injury—something that required surgery— he wouldn't have been able to sleep so soundly. He'd have a worsening headache. He'd said the simple pain reliever had helped and the fact that he was several hours past his injury without any neurological signs proved there wasn't a major bleed in his head.

Then why the amnesia? Was it more than just trauma related? Some patients developed amnesia from psychological stress. Was this the driving force in Casper's case? If so, how could she help him?

They neared the house. The sun had set. They'd been driving on an old jeep trail for about an hour. The washboard ruts culled Casper from sleep. In the dim moonlight, he did look better to her. More alert. A quiet attentiveness.

The house was hidden in a grove of trees. Casper instructed her to drive into them, to hide the car from the view of the road—if you could call it that.

"Don't park close to the house. Let's get farther back into the trees."

Ashley did as instructed and parked the car. They sat there staring at the structure for the longest time, neither of them saying a word. It was an average-sized log cabin. It felt familiar to Ashley, though she couldn't remember any particular visit. The moon gave the forest a faint yellowish glow and the only things that stirred were quick black flecks as mice scurried over the snow scavenging for food.

"I feel like I've been here before," Casper said, his voice soft…almost haunted.

"Me, too. Are we waiting for something?" Ashley asked, eyes still locked on the structure. When had she been here? Had her mother been with her? Seemingly she hadn't been old enough for a solid memory to have formed.

"Movement of something more than mice."

The house was dark. Even at this distance, it exuded a silence that made Ashley feel like no one had been here in a while. The snow was undisturbed. Leaves were heaped in piles near one side of the doorway. In the front yard, tipped over and broken, was an old birdbath.

"I need to show you something," Ashley said, turning and grabbing the manila envelope that sat on the back seat. Returning forward, she pressed the button for the dome light, and then thumbed through the photos she'd gotten at various times in different packages. Thankfully, she'd been keeping these together at work.

There it was, proof in black-and-white, the house at a time when it appeared much more glorious than it did now.

She held the photo up to the light so Casper could see it, as well. "It's the same cabin."

"If your father sent these then I'm hopeful it's confirmation that we're in the right place. I can't help but think there must be more to the photos than that. More clues than what is obvious."

Ashley tapped her fingers against the top of the pile. "This photo of the cabin was the first one I got." She flipped it over. "It has a number on the back." Ashley reordered the stack of photos. "The next three photos also had numbers on the back."

"Each was sent at a different time?"

"Yes. The four numbers together are 8519."

"Do they mean anything to you?" Casper asked.

"Not to me. You?"

Casper tapped his index finger against his temple. "Still pretty foggy up here."

"We'll freeze out here if we sit too long," Ashley said as she reached for the door handle. Casper eased his hand over hers, enveloping hers in a warm, comforting hold. Her heart jumped slightly at his unexpected touch. He didn't say anything, and in the low light, shadows cast over his face, she couldn't discern any meaning from the touch, but to her it conveyed camaraderie…safety.

A commitment that they were in this thing—whatever this thing was—together.

As she watched him, her heart fluttering lightly at the base of her throat, he nodded his head as if to affirm something in his mind, and he relinquished her hand. He opened his car door and she did the same.

They walked parallel to the front of the house, the snow crystals splitting under their feet one of the few sounds in the night. Casper approached the door first and tested the knob. It didn't make sense to Ashley, but seemed subconscious in a way. He also held his right hand near his hip, like a law enforcement officer would, keeping his palm on the hilt of a sidearm. Muscle memory she guessed. If she was right, what type of law enforcement did he do?

Casper felt along the edges of the door. To Ashley, it appeared to be a normal locked door. He waved at her to follow and they began searching around the house. She didn't quite know what he was looking for so she simply looked for something obviously out of place.

The house just seemed old and unused.

On the back of the property, there was a large screened-in porch. Casper opened the door onto the portico with ease, but stood there for endless seconds as if waiting for something. Ashley held her breath. Every minute sound of the forest caused her skin to prickle. Casper waved her onto the stoop and they neared the back door. It, too, was locked. Casper began scanning the back wall when he found something out of the ordinary.

Looking closely, at eye level, there seemed to be a small window cut into the side of the house. Casper turned a simple closure and opened a door that was no more than six by six inches. On the inside of the door there was a punch code lock.

Could that be what the numbers were for on the back of those photos?

Casper seemed to have the same idea as he punched the numbers in the sequence Ashley had gotten on the photos.

Nothing.

"Try it backward," Ashley suggested.

He did and a cover popped open.

Casper stepped back. Ashley's nerves tingled. "What is that?"

"I think it's a security device based on facial recognition."

Ashley took two steps back. Who was her father, really? A facial scanner? In a cabin in the woods? Someplace she felt like she'd been before.

A viridian set of eyes looked back at her with three flashing red words.

Ready to scan.

"You first," Ashley said. "Then if it's a booby trap maybe I can save your life."

"That's ridiculous. They don't work that way."

"All of a sudden a man who can't remember who he is becomes an expert in facial scanners and booby traps?"

"It's just like a camera. No lasers. It won't hurt you."

"You were almost beat into an early grave. I saw a good friend get shot right in front of me. I called Horace. The next risky move is all yours."

"Fine." Casper stepped in front of the screen. Within a few seconds it flashed. *Access denied.*

Ashley shuddered. It was cold and this was creepy. What had she gotten herself involved in? This was straight out of a James Bond movie.

Before she could change her mind, she walked up to the window and stood stock-still until the device flashed.

Access granted.

There was a faint pop of a door releasing and Casper walked quickly through the back porch door. The interior was dark but they could see another doorway at the end. Leading the way, she walked forward and they were met with another punch code lock.

Ashley entered the numbers backward. No luck this time. She tried forward.

Another window popped open. Ashley repeated the same maneuvers.

Access denied.

She stepped away from the door. "Now what do we do?"

Casper stepped forward without acknowledging her question. After scanning Casper's face, the door released.

What did that mean? That they only would have been given entry if they were together?

Casper stepped through the threshold and motioned

her forward and turned on a series of light switches as he walked.

The interior of the cabin was an entirely different story. It didn't look old and untouched, but fairly modernized.

Had her father been here sometime in the past two years? Did her mother remember this place?

The first thing that stood out was the movie projector in the middle of the room facing a white wall.

"Should we turn it on?" Ashley asked.

"Seems like we're meant to."

SIX

Casper's feet were heavy, his hunger forgotten, as he neared the projector. What could this be? After a quick inspection, he turned the dial and the projector was set in motion. Ashley sat down on a worn leather love seat. Casper remained standing. He wanted to be able to turn the video off if something too disturbing came on the screen.

There was no sound, just grainy images with streaked black lines running through the frames. Color but faded. The first shot was of an island taken a good distance away. Next, men were loading sheep into a small boat— a wooden boat with oars.

If Casper had to guess the time frame, based on the dress alone, he'd say 1930s to 1940s. In the next few scenes, the sheep were being placed in small metal pens. Each animal was individually locked in these cages. Then a tan, canvas-type hood was placed over the sheep's head.

A long view then showed several of the crates on a hillside.

Men in biohazard gear. Orange suits. Canvas hoods. Old-style respirators. Close to the style of gas masks worn by WWI soldiers.

A queasy feeling hit Casper. He was starting to feel

light-headed and decided it might be best to sit next to Ashley on the couch. This was not a first-date kind of movie night he expected to take any woman on.

Another long view of the hillside. The sheep remained in the crates. A plane flew over dropping something from its cargo hold.

A bomb.

That didn't explode.

A plume of brown smoke wafted over the hill.

Casper's throat thickened. It was difficult to breathe, as if the mysterious smoke was filling the small cabin.

Next few screen images. The sheep were unloaded from the crates and tied to long metal poles anchored in the ground. Time passes. Three days according to an informational placard.

The sheep all died.

Then necropsies. Ashley shielded her eyes. Sometimes, even medical doctors had a limit as to what they could watch. Casper hustled to the film and turned it off.

"What was that?" Ashley asked, slowly revealing her eyes from the protective cover of her hand.

"Gruinard Island…if I had to guess," Casper said.

"This film footage…was a real event? Not some cut of a low-budget horror movie left on the editing floor?"

"There have been a couple of islands known to be used for military experiments of bioweapons. The Brits had Gruinard Island. The Russians had Rebirth Island. I think this is Gruinard because the Russians favored using monkeys in their testing."

Ashley leaned her head against the back of the love seat. "Your memory seems to be improving."

Casper nodded. He was remembering more, but it was like a fast unloading of this life. He could clearly remember high school, his family and going through college.

Microbiology. He had a clear picture of holding an acceptance letter to medical school in his hands.

He'd been fascinated by bioweapons—the destructive power of something infinitely smaller than its foe.

"Yes, I am remembering more," Casper said.

"Why didn't you say anything to me?"

"We've been busy."

"We were on the road for hours… You couldn't find one moment?" she asked, her tone accusatory.

Casper's hackles rose, but before he responded with the same tone he considered her perspective. There was likely a trust issue at play here. Her father had abandoned her family, and yet he was, more likely than not, still alive. If her father was alive but not engaged, why couldn't he just be honest with her? It seemed to Casper that Ashley wanted the truth more than anything else—despite the pain it might cause.

It was always the hidden things that drove people crazy. The truth, though hard, at least could be managed, rebuilt from and moved past.

Casper inhaled to ease the tinge of anger in his chest. Ultimately, they had to trust one another. If there was suspicion between them, it was only going to hurt them in the long run.

"I'm sorry. What I was remembering didn't seem to have any particular significance until now."

She looked at him, a softness to her face. He'd been forgiven even if she couldn't say the words. "What did we just watch?"

"In my college years, I was pretty fascinated by this stuff. I'd done some reading about biological weapons programs and knew about these islands. There were reports that footage of Gruinard Island had been declassified, but I'd never seen the footage."

"You think this is the original?"

Casper shrugged. "Hard to know. I would guess a copy. Not sure why it hasn't been converted into something digital. Or maybe it has, but your father didn't want to risk a digital footprint by having it on a computer."

"What biological agent was that?"

"That was anthrax. Inhaled anthrax spores are fatal in 90 percent of cases." Casper rested his hand on top of the projector. "You can see from the film they wanted to ensure inhalation of the spores to determine lethality. That's why the sheep's heads are covered. The hoods diminish cross-contamination between the animals. The crude necropsies verify the cause of death. Really, though terrible, this is a perfectly designed experiment. Even the time of day they dropped the bomb."

Ashley's eyes glanced up to the ceiling. "Dusk?"

"Yes. Minimal sunlight. Some pathogens will die when exposed to UV light, but nightfall is when it's more likely that cool air will cover warm…inversion. It keeps the spores from being blown away by wind currents. By the slight breeze as seen in the taller grasses, the plume is carried toward the sheep as the men stand upwind."

Ashley leaned forward and rubbed her forehead with her fingers as if staving off a headache. "It always amazes me."

"What?"

"Man's desire to kill one another."

He couldn't offer a counterargument.

"Why do you think my father left it for us?"

"To start us down the right path. Bioweapons. One or both of us has information that this Jared Fleming is probably involved in, or something along these lines. Your father left us a film reel dealing with a biological weapons experiment. Why? I don't know…yet. Let's look around and see what else we find."

Ashley stood from the couch on shaky legs and headed for the desk. Casper looked through cabinets in the kitchen. Didn't seem like the best place to find clues to their current predicament, but she was also getting hungry.

She pulled open a drawer that held a series of files. Grabbing the first one, she set it on the desk and flipped it open. It was filled with a series of codes.

"Ravioli?" Casper asked. "There's nothing but canned goods here. I can add green beans."

"In it?" Ashley asked. Her stomach clenched at the thought. She wasn't a food snob, but neither did her stomach have the same stalwart intestinal fortitude of her youth. Yet canned ravioli had been one of her favorite things. Was this an olive branch extended by her father for her arrival? Having the cabinets stocked with some of her favorite foods from her childhood?

"Really? You have to ask me that?"

His smile lightened Ashley's spirits. "Just checking. My brother is known to eat some pretty interesting things that he's tried to innocently pass off to me."

Ashley turned back to the papers as Casper continued in the kitchen, looking for something to warm up their dinner. She heard the whine of an electric can opener. After a few dishes were shuffled, she heard Casper program the microwave and the faint hum of it starting.

Whatever this place was, someone was paying to keep the power connected.

Casper walked next to her. "Find anything?"

"These codes." Ashley pointed to the stack of documents. "Do you know what they might mean?"

Casper lifted the paper from the top of the desk. "These are the Soviet classification codes for their bio-weapons program. Each number and letter combination represents an agent."

"How would you know that?" Ashley asked.

"A Russian scientist who defected to the US after the fall of the Soviet Union wrote a book about it. He was a high-ranking military scientist that was in charge of their weapons program."

Ashley took the paper from his fingers and set it back on the desk. "Decipher them for me."

"Well, I didn't memorize them from his autobiography, but the Russians had a love affair with the most virulent pathogens. There wasn't anything they didn't consider or try weaponizing—smallpox, Ebola and anthrax were just a few they tinkered with. In fact, they had an accidental release of anthrax that killed quite a few citizens."

Accidental? Could it really be called that if the government was testing something that was against international law? *Criminal* seemed to be the more appropriate term.

Casper continued, "And even a second round of deaths when they tried to clean it up."

"How could something like that happen?"

"Anthrax spores are very hardy. In the film we saw, Gruinard Island was considered a biological wasteland for decades. To clean up the spores, they sprayed the soil with a combination of formaldehyde and seawater before it was considered anthrax free. Regular cleanup, like spraying an area with water and soap, can just disperse the spores into the air, where they can turn around and infect additional people."

The microwave pinged drawing Casper back to the kitchen. "See what else you can find and I'll get dinner set up."

Ashley put her attention back to the file cabinet to the right of the desk and thumbed through the tabs. Variant U. India 1967. Anthrax 836. Unit 731. What were these and why had her father been stockpiling information on them?

There was a small hope chest against the wall to the left of where she sat. Ashley left the desk and kneeled next to the intricately carved camphor trunk. They came from China if she remembered correctly. This one was etched with complex designs—dragons, pagodas and sailing ships. Ashley trailed her fingers over the wood. She remembered her father bringing one of these home to her mother after a lengthy trip and it was one of her mother's most treasured gifts.

Ashley lifted the lock and was greeted by a smell that reminded her of the ointment her mother used to spread on her chest as a child with the cursory placement of wax paper over top to keep the substance from saturating her pajamas. Her mother claimed the smell was like rosemary but Ashley disagreed. A tear slipped from her eye and she quickly wiped it away.

Lord, Casper seems to believe in You and that You're the ultimate composer of life. That everything has a time, a place and a purpose. I don't know why these things are happening to us, but I'm scared. Keep my mother and brother safe. Continue to allow Casper to regain his memory. Help us decipher these clues so that we can find my father...alive.

She pushed the lid fully open. The first thing that caught her attention was a gray-and-black toolbox. Her father used these to make up complex first-aid kits. After she pulled it out, she set it next to her on the floor and opened it up.

The top tray held smaller items—Band-Aids, cotton

balls, antibiotic ointment, ACE wraps and one tightly folded Mylar blanket. How those things could keep anyone warm was questionable. She lifted the top of the tray and found two bags of IV fluid, several packages of IV tubing and IV catheters of various sizes. More bandages and different types of medical tape took up the remainder of the space. She lifted out some of the larger bandages and found three prescription bottles tucked underneath. Grabbing them, she turned back toward the desk light to read the labels.

Her father's cryptic block lettering had fashioned a homemade label.

Tetracycline. Penicillin. Streptomycin.

Three potent antibiotics.

All used to treat diseases that could result from a biological weapons attack.

SEVEN

Casper lit the last of a trio of small tea lights he found in one of the cabinets and surveyed the table setting in front of him. A plate of ravioli and green beans...from a can. He was definitely failing on all levels of any first-date criteria.

Is that what I'm trying to do here? Impress Ashley... romantically?

He looked at her across the room as she rummaged through the old chest that sat next to her father's desk. Surprisingly, she didn't look as disheveled as he thought she would under the circumstances. Her ponytail had been transformed into a messy bun. Small wisps of her dark brown hair fought the confines of the holder and framed her face. She could use some sun; her skin was as light and pale as paper, with a hint of pink at her cheeks. No makeup marred her complexion and she was still stunningly beautiful. Those blue eyes always inquisitive yet tentative—like she didn't want to let any man get too close.

"Dinner's ready," Casper called to her, his heartbeat upticking as she stood and faced him. She took two steps and stopped. She held something in her hands but he couldn't tell what it was.

Her head tilted in question as she began to walk to the table. "Candles?"

Casper pulled the torn vinyl seat, straight from the '70s, out for her to sit down on. "Probably not wise for us to turn on a bunch of lights," Casper said. "We are trying to keep a low profile."

She positioned herself in front of the chair and Casper gently pushed it underneath her. He took two steps to her side and unfolded a thin paper napkin and placed it on her lap. "Just because we're on the run from some nefarious people doesn't mean we need to live uncivilized."

Ashley chuckled and the pressure eased from his chest. "No, of course not. I guess."

Casper reached for her hand across the table and Ashley returned hers in kind, resting her fingers lightly in his palm. He gripped them gently. His memory was slowly coming up to the current time period. He remembered his residency and then choosing to specialize in infectious disease. From that time span, he couldn't remember a girlfriend and was beginning to wonder if he'd had a serious love interest in this life before.

"Dear Lord. We don't understand the circumstances under which You brought Ashley and I together. Each of us seems to hold pieces of a puzzle and we need Your help to see the big picture. Give us the tools to decipher and see clearly what is before us. Please return the use of my memory, but only if it is Your will. Amen."

Casper slid his hand out from underneath Ashley's and found her blue eyes locked on his as soon as he looked up. He reached for his face, thinking he had a spot of spaghetti sauce running rogue somewhere from eating one extra ravioli.

"There's nothing there," Ashley said.

"It's just that…you're staring," Casper said. "I'm feeling a little scrutinized."

Ashley picked up her fork and waved it in front of him as if to brush the thought aside. "I'm sorry, it's just that I'm a little intrigued by your prayer."

The nervous tingle returned to Casper's chest. Was Ashley always this way? So direct? Perhaps it was a skill developed in the ER. If you weren't to the point, lives could be lost. "In what way?"

"Thy will be done. How could it not be God's will for your memory to return?"

Casper took his olive green plastic cup and sipped his water slowly. He didn't know if he had the wherewithal at this point in time to have a theological discussion. "God's will is what I strive for. Sometimes God doesn't give us the things we want so He can show us His presence in our lives."

Ashley scooped another ravioli, remaining silent for a few minutes. "How else will we find the clues we need unless you can remember who is after you and why?"

Casper shrugged. "I don't know, Ashley. I can only take the next step that is in front of me. When I was doing my medical training, it always seemed to be the ER types who wanted to control chaos. The obsessive ones. What I see in working in infectious disease is that once the infection hits, we are reactionary to the process. We have an arsenal in place—we can try this and that antibiotic, but we have to wait and see how the patient progresses. Sometimes, I think God acts in this way. He gives us an obstacle and then waits to see what we do with it. Do we depend on ourselves or do we depend on Him?"

Ashley took a few bites, seemingly considering his words. "Seems like a big cosmic game to me."

Casper swallowed more water as he considered her point.

Ashley pointed to the bottles she brought from the first-aid kit to the table. "Next to the desk there is a big first-aid kit. In the bottom were these antibiotics."

No further discussion on God was on the table.

Casper eyed the labels and popped open the top of one, shuffling the pills inside. "These are common for treating certain biological agents. Anthrax and tularemia."

"I've never seen a case of tularemia even though it's supposed to be present in the Rocky Mountain region."

"It's probably not the most sought-after biological weapon, but it looks like your father was planning for several contingencies."

"Did you check the expiration dates on this can of ravioli?" Ashley asked.

"Of course. I'm an infectious disease doctor. Botulism is something I definitely don't want to contract. Does it taste funny to you?"

Ashley spooned the last bite into her mouth. Evidently not. She'd eaten the whole bowl and was now chasing the green beans with her spoon. She smiled. "No. In fact, it's the best thing I've tasted in a long time."

"Stress and hunger will do that to you," Casper said, finishing the last bite of his green beans. "What else did you find?"

"Enough supplies to treat a fairly decent medical emergency. IV supplies. Fluids even."

That intrigued Casper. It wasn't that a doctor shouldn't be prepared, but it was rare to carry supplies to start a field IV. From the looks of the interior of the cabin, someone hadn't been here in a while—a year perhaps seemed reasonable, but it also didn't look like the cabin had been abandoned for decades, either.

"Are the fluids expired?" Casper asked.

"I didn't check."

"I think we should rummage through this cabin and put some supplies in the car to take with us," Casper said.

"Why do you ask?"

"About what?"

"About the expiration date on the fluids."

"I'm just trying to determine a time frame for when Russell might have been here. A bag of IV fluids is good for a couple of years."

"So he could have dropped by in the last year or so," Ashley said.

"Yes, probably—sometime after his disappearance two years ago?"

Ashley smoothed her tongue over her teeth. "You're remembering more?"

Quick change of topic. She was astute, that was for sure. "Through school. It's like the tape of my life is being played by my memory in forward motion. I still don't know how I met your father, or what we were doing when that photo was taken. Seemingly, whatever work he was involved in deals with biological weapons."

"Where do we go next?" Ashley asked.

"I think we need to take a look at all the clues your father sent you."

Ashley got up from the table to retrieve the package. When she turned away, Casper placed four Oreo cookies on her plate.

When she returned, she almost seemed entranced by the treats. "Where did you get these?"

"In the cabinet. I tried a few and I haven't died yet."

"This whole cabin is strange for me. My father stocked it with all my favorite things." Ashley grabbed a cookie and held it up. "With these, he always insisted on eating the center first."

Casper smiled. "Well, he was a smart man. Seems to be the way I like Oreos, too."

He watched her as she enjoyed the treat. It amazed him how people could enjoy the simple things in life even in the midst of a crisis. After eating her cookies, she was unusually quiet, as if considering a course of action.

"What's on your mind?" he asked. "You seem to be mulling something over."

"I just feel like we're operating in the dark. I don't even know what our next step is going to be."

"I saw a radio in one of the cabinets. Let's turn it on. After that, we'll do a more thorough analysis of the items your father sent you."

Ashley held her breath as Casper turned the dial. Even in the middle of the woods they were able to find an AM radio station. They listened through the droll of news and weather when a local shock jock started the hour with what he termed his mystery of the week.

Of which Ashley was at the top of the list.

"Colorado State Police are on the hunt for an Aurora-based emergency room physician by the name of Ashley Drager. They're not claiming she's armed and dangerous, but I honestly don't know what you'd consider her after the trail of mayhem she's left behind."

Every bit of strength Ashley had been holding on to leached from her body. Casper laid a gentle hand on her shoulder and eased her onto the torn, fractured leather love seat. He held the radio as he sat next to her. Another sign her father had likely been to the cabin in the last couple of years—the batteries to the radio still worked. Casper placed the radio on his lap. A small kindness she was thankful for considering how much she was trembling.

I save lives...and now they suspect me of being involved in harming others.

The radio host continued, "I mean, this CCTV footage of the security guard getting shot as he tries to stop her from taking a patient from the hospital is pretty amazing. He's still in critical condition. You can find the grisly scene on our web page. Doesn't look like she fired the shot, but could be that she's in cahoots with the person who did. Can you believe the hospital released this? We still don't know what happened to the patient she took... The hospital is claiming patient privacy issues even though the police have released the image of this man, Casper English, in hopes of garnering information on his whereabouts."

Ashley's throat dried. Her lungs burned from holding her breath at each utterance of the man's words. At least Noah was still alive...for the time being. If they didn't straighten this mess out—and they didn't even know what it was—she may never be able to practice medicine again. Her father's life seemed over...and now so would hers be.

She began to cry. Tiredness washed over her and she leaned her head back against the couch. There could be no God in this...in ruining the life of an innocent person.

Casper wrapped his arm around her shoulders and pulled her close. She rested her head against his chest. Immediately, the strength he exuded calmed her anxiety. Her breathing slowed. It was the safest she'd felt in a long time.

"Do you want me to turn it off?" he asked.

She shook her head. They were already in the dark. Even though this truth might be painful to hear, she had to know what she was being accused of.

"First the patient, then the security guard and now she's being implicated in the murder of one Horace Longbottom."

At those words, Casper gripped her shoulder tightly as her body started to shake again.

"Security footage from a local grocery store shows Longbottom picking up the duo outside. In-store CCTV shows—can you believe this?—of all things she's buying coffee, and then the guy ends up dead within forty-eight hours of their meeting. Men, stay away from this woman—this so-called healer. Looks like all she brings is death. Might fit the definition of a true lady killer. Notify law enforcement if you sight her, but stay a safe distance away."

Now it just wasn't Jared looking for them, but law enforcement and local citizens.

Casper turned the radio off and set it on the floor. He pulled Ashley closer with both arms and took one hand to smooth her hair.

There was no coming back from this. She was ruined.

"We will figure this out," Casper tried to reassure her.

"How?" she questioned through her tears.

"I don't know that. It's not clear to me, but what is clear is that we're in this together. I'm not going to abandon you no matter what that means for me."

Things like this didn't happen to real people, and yet here she was, smack in the middle of the biggest trauma and mystery of her life. Her father disappearing had been nothing compared to this. They had painted her as a ruthless murderess.

"What I do know is that you need rest. You've been taking care of me. Now it's time for me to return the favor." He stood up and held his hand out. She took it reluctantly as he guided her to the only bedroom with a small bathroom. He went to the bed and pulled down the log cabin quilt made with rich autumn colors by her mother's hands. Her thoughts shifted to her mother's safety.

Casper eased her toward the bed until she sat down.

"We won't be able to think through this if we're both exhausted. You've been driving all day and that is a drain on your mind."

"What are you going to do?" Ashley asked.

"Spend some more time looking around the cabin and gather some stuff that might be handy in the car. Then I'll sleep for a while on the couch. This might be the safest we are in the near term so no hurry in the morning, but we can't stay here another full day. I think it's too risky. Hopefully something between now and then will give us our next step."

Ashley watched him close the door. She stepped into the bathroom and rummaged around. When she looked under the bottom of the sink, she found all the toiletries she'd used in her childhood, still sealed. Again, nothing had expired, but it was also like her relationship with her father was frozen in time—like she was constantly the age of ten in his mind.

She leaned against the bathroom counter and let the tears fall. How had her life gotten so wildly out of control? Paired up with a man she didn't know and on the run for her life? Her father had seemingly sent her the clues that could save her, yet right now, they were mostly undecipherable.

Ashley brushed her teeth with the berry-flavored glitter toothpaste and gagged at the taste. Adulthood had morphed her taste buds into something that could no longer stand the sweetness. She went back into the small bedroom. There was a desk with a laptop. She neared it.

Again, not the most recent model, but purchased in the last couple of years. It wasn't marred or dented, and when she raised the top the keys looked untouched. No food particles were present in the crevices. She looked at the side and found two USB ports, and her hand itched to insert the thumb drive into one, but fatigue overwhelmed her and ultimately she had to agree with Casper's assessment.

Before lying in the bed she looked out the window. There was a black box just beyond it, partially covered in snow. It seemed out of place for the woods and there was a red light that blinked every so often. Too tired to consider investigating it now, she lay down on the bed and pulled the covers over her, the faint smell of her mother's perfume in the fabric a comfort.

When she slept, all she dreamed about were sheep dying on a hillside.

EIGHT

Casper was awakened by a stream of light crossing his eyes. He blinked rapidly, disoriented, his heart racing.

A cabin in the woods. He had a headache and he reached for his face, the bumps somewhat less prominent but the residual trauma still painful.

Ashley.

He looked toward the door. It was still closed. He groped for what he assumed to be something that would tell time. A watch or a cell phone—neither of which he had. The wind whistled softly through the gaps around the door. He turned on the radio and waited until they mentioned the time. Seven o'clock.

Relief washed over him. He hadn't slept half the day away. He wanted him and Ashley to get away from this site. Every minute could draw the assassins closer to their location. He eyed the small sidearm he'd found in one of the closets and tucked it into the waistband of his jeans as he stood up.

Mild dizziness overtook him and he pressed his fingers to his forehead.

A memory thrust forward in his mind. He remembered first meeting Ashley's father.

So they did know one another on a personal level. The

recollection was no more than a flash, but it was also comforting. Casper had been reaching across a patient's bed, the beginning of his infectious disease fellowship, and had shook hands with Dr. Russell Drager.

The thought faded. Another retelling of his life in slow motion. He tried to recall any details of the anamnesis that might help him in his current situation...and nothing.

He'd stayed up perhaps two hours after Ashley had gone to bed, scouring the cabin for anything that might help them: a first-aid kit, various food items and several gallons of water. It was hard to predict where this road would take them next, but he wanted to plan for as many different contingencies as possible.

Another thing he found—a CDC badge with his credentials. Had he worked for the Centers for Disease Control? Was it a fake?

Regardless, he'd stowed it in the car, as well. It could prove useful.

Straightening his clothes, he approached Ashley's door and knocked softly. To his surprise, she was awake and called for him to come in. He found her standing in front of the computer in the room. She looked at him sheepishly and he took two more steps inside.

"I haven't been completely honest with you," she said, her hands stuffed into the pockets of her jeans.

At first, his chest clenched with disappointment, but then how could he blame her? Her father was missing under mysterious circumstances. She didn't know Casper, truly. He could be as dangerous as the men who chased them. But something in her body language, in her eyes and the way she looked at him had changed—perhaps *softened* was the better term. Less guarded. Like maybe she was venturing forward with a small modicum of trust.

"It's okay. It's not hard for me to understand why."

She studied him and it was hard for him not to admire just how pretty she was. Her hair was slightly tousled from sleep, but her eyes were clear, strikingly blue, just like the waters off Belize where he'd scuba dived once on college spring break.

"I want to show you something."

She beckoned him to the other side of the bed to the small window that looked out onto the west side of the property. It was a black box, hope chest size. Looked newish, but essentially undisturbed. There weren't any footprints around it. In the shade of the cabin he could see a red light blinking.

"You've not seen it before?" he asked her.

"No, but I haven't been here since I was young. Like elementary school. What do you think it could be?" she asked.

"I have no idea. A storage bin? Guess we should go take a look in it before we leave. Seems strange…out of place, but it hasn't killed us yet."

Ashley paused and looked at him strangely.

"That's not funny."

"What?"

"You're forecasting," Ashley said.

"As in the weather?"

"No. You're doing what patients do. They'll say something ominous yet with a sense of humor, but inside they're scared about it. Oftentimes, the thing they joked about comes true. Such as, 'Well, it hasn't killed me yet.' And then that's exactly what happens."

Casper didn't know what to say. Was he subconsciously worried about the bin?

She tossed something small and plastic onto the desk. A thumb drive. "This is the last thing my father sent to me. It arrived the same day you did."

He neared it and picked it up, fingering it, almost hoping the information would transfer automatically to his mind. This seemed like the obvious next step, to put this drive into the computer and see what it held, but he was nervous. He couldn't quite pinpoint where this feeling was coming from, but it felt intuitive. Still, what choice did they have? Neither of them really knew where to go next.

"I think we should see what's on it."

"Me, too," she agreed and took it from his hand, her fingertips soft against his calloused skin.

Ashley turned the computer on and they waited until the desktop icons were present. She inserted the thumb drive and Casper's stomach gnawed at his insides while he waited for the computer to recognize the drive.

Up on the screen came an image of a black skull dripping blood.

Needles of fear zipped through Casper's body. He raced to the window, where the red flashing light was now a solid green.

"It's a trap!" he yelled and raced back to the computer. He grabbed the thumb drive and the stack of photos as he reached for Ashley's hand and made moves to extract her from the cabin.

She resisted him. "Casper, wait."

"No, I mean it. Run!"

He pulled her behind him as he broke into a sprint toward the front door. Her footsteps faltered behind him, as if she questioned if they were in any danger.

They were through the door, their feet puffing up snow as they raced to the car, when a blast wave traveled through Casper's body, jolting every internal organ. His body was falling before the flash of fire flamed over him like an inferno exhaling. For a few seconds, he was airborne, remnants of the cabin pelting him like a violent hailstorm. Ashley's hand was yanked from his, and he moved his arms forward to break the coming fall. He landed, hard, on his stomach, his limbs coming to rest in the snow. Pine trees splitting cracked in small explosions. Casper rolled onto his back. A roil of black smoke shot upward to the sky.

Someone had set a trap at Russell's cabin, but for whom?

He couldn't breathe. Each small breath was like a popped flare in his chest. A tall tree next to him swayed threateningly, as if teasing that death could still claim him. Casper forced himself to take deeper breaths. Wiggling his fingers and toes, he confirmed that his nerves were still intact and operating under his brain's central command. As he struggled to sit up, his previous injures ached and his vision tilted with a serious bout of vertigo. He placed a hand down onto the forest floor to steady himself until the scene before him was steady.

Desperately, he scanned the ground for Ashley. Where was she? The cabin was disintegrating, its skeleton food for the hungry blaze. All that would be left was smoldering ash when its appetite was satiated.

"Casper…"

At first, upon hearing his whispered name, he thought his mind was playing tricks on him to convince himself that she was still alive because he couldn't see her anywhere.

A cough made him turn around. Still, he didn't see anything.

Until he looked up.

There she was, seemingly cradled in a tree branch like a mother holding an infant. In disbelief, he settled on his knees and tried to come to terms with her predicament. His heart thumped wildly as he watched her closed eyes.

His mind begged them to open—to see that blue lively and engaged.

And then he saw it, the faint but rapid rise of her chest. She was alive.

He scurried to his feet and raced toward the tree. She was not far up into the branches. Her hand dangled down at about shoulder height, and he took it between both of his. It was cold, her fingertips blue.

"Ashley…" he said, as he sneaked his fingers into the groove of her wrist to assess her pulse. It was weak, barely palpable. Too fast.

Her eyes opened and her gaze wandered aimlessly around her—the blue of her irises fractured by the heightened red trails of the veins against her sclera. What normally appeared white was now a spiderweb of red. Her inability to focus and engage him was a clear sign of shock—but from what? It was important for him to determine the injury to treat her appropriately.

"Ashley," he said with more conviction. Finally her eyes locked on his and he stepped closer to the tree. "What hurts?"

She squeezed her eyes, her lips made a few motions, but no words were verbalized. He moved his hand up to her shoulder and brought the other one to her chest, feeling her breaths beneath his palm. He didn't need a watch to know how fast they were. Briefly, he rested his chin against his shoulder to organize his thoughts.

What do I do, Lord? If I move her without knowing the extent of her injuries, I could kill her. I don't want her to die.

Clenching his teeth against the thought, he looked back at her. "Ashley, wiggle your fingers and toes." He could see her fingers move faintly and when he placed his hand over her tennis shoes, he could feel her toes wiggle under the canvas.

There was a low branch on the tree that seemed broad enough to support his weight, and he stepped on it to get closer to her. With one hand, he reached behind and felt her neck, and he didn't perceive any bony abnormalities. On gross observation, her spinal cord seemed intact.

She tried to lift her head, but then it dropped back, her eyes closed. Everything about her body signified that she might be trying to leave it.

"Ashley," he called to her. Nothing. He pinched her fingertip, hard, to see if she would respond to the pain. "Ashley!" Again, no response. His heartbeat faltered, his throat was tight and he placed two fingers at her neck in search of a pulse.

There was one, and she was still breathing, but her lips were dusky, and if he didn't do something right now, he was going to lose her.

With one hand behind her neck, and the other scooping under her lower back, he pulled her toward him.

She didn't come forward.

Something tethered her to the trunk. Casper clenched his eyes. He knew in his mind every medical reason not to jerk her body from the tree, but he was running out of time and he couldn't do anything for her medically while she was hanging from a branch.

With all his might, he pulled again and she came free, her body falling into his chest. The momentum carried him backward and he quickly placed a foot on the ground to steady himself before he dropped her. Something wet trickled onto his hand that supported her back.

Blood.

Looking back at the tree, he saw what had happened.

A short, spear-like branch had impaled her. But where? Had he just killed her by removing her from it?

He went to his knees and set her on the ground. A faint moan escaped her lips, and though he was sorrowful for the amount of pain she must be in, he also rejoiced because it meant she was still with him.

Turning her away from him, he lifted up the back of her shirt. A small stream of blood flowed from a wound just under her right shoulder blade. Now everything made sense. Likely, her lung was punctured and the only way to save her life was to put a chest tube in.

Turning her back toward him, he picked her back up and ran to the car.

A hot poker seared Ashley's side. Her eyes popped open and she felt a reassuring hand cup her cheek.

"Shh, it's all right. We're safe. For now."

Her vision was blurry. Her hands reached toward her right side to feel what was causing the intense pain, but Casper held her hand tightly in his. "You have a chest tube."

If that were true, what should greet her clearing vision were the bright lights of a hospital room. Instead, a musty odor filled her nostrils. She could see rafters, a dark, cabin-like interior, complete with cobwebs and a mounted deer head on the wall.

A hunting cabin?

She turned her head toward his voice and he sat next to her on a wooden stool. She was lying on a threadbare floral couch. The colors were reminiscent of something from the '70s that would most likely be found on the side of the road with a "free" cardboard sign perched on the cushions. She was half covered in an olive green wool blanket with holes in various spots. Small, anemic flames wiggled in a woodstove a few feet from the base of the couch.

Beyond her was a table. On it were an old gas can and a few wire hangers. There were discarded bags of IV fluids. She felt the crook of her right arm and there was an IV in place, but nothing connected at this time. Somehow, Casper had jury-rigged together a chest tube from gas pump siphon tubing, likely the end set in something that held water. As if reading her thoughts, Casper picked up a large mason jar, where the end of the red tubing sat. Small air bubbles intermittently floated to the surface.

Setting it back down, he grabbed a glass of water and held out a few pills in one palm.

"You need to take these. It's some of the penicillin we found. I can't say I exactly used a 100 percent sterile technique when I put the tube in to help your lung reexpand. Sorry to say, there's nothing stronger than Tylenol and ibuprofen in the kit for the pain. Want some?"

She nodded. It was something she wasn't going to disagree with him about. He shook four blue gel capsules from a bottle and helped her sit up, and she swallowed them. Her stomach began to cramp as he settled her back onto the throng of old pillows he'd scavenged from the cabin. His face was awash with relief. The deep creases in his forehead relaxed. An impish smile made his dimples prominent. It was relief but also pride. She'd probably feel the same way saving someone's life under such adverse conditions.

Slowly, the events that had brought them to this place came forward in her mind. The explosion. A tree. Not too much after that. Never again could she justify doubting a patient's story when it came to traumatic injury. Being impaled by a tree after an explosion? She'd definitely have to cut her ER clientele some slack.

Ashley glanced down at her chest and noticed her shirt had been cut up the side. Her fingers traveled up the row of black buttons, noting the top three were open, revealing the uppermost portion of her scar that was visible at the break.

That meant he knew… He had to know.

He caught her eye as she looked up. "Want to tell me about your heart surgery?"

She gathered the shirt closer to her neck. "Two holes in my heart. I was in elementary school when they were repaired."

"Anything I should know…medically speaking?"

Those had been hard days for her family. They were financially strapped for money. At the time, she'd heard her parents argue over words she didn't understand. *Debt. Foreclosure.* Arguments over the right timing of her surgery and how they were going to withstand the medical bills. Ashley had felt guilty that her condition was causing them so much stress. However, none of those things had come to fruition. Somehow, they'd patched things together for Ashley to get her procedure—even moving into a larger house within the year.

"No, it hasn't been an issue."

He covered her hands with his. "That's good to know. I'd hate to…"

Lose you? Are those the words he meant to say but left out?

"How many days have we been here?"

"Two."

She inhaled deeply. How was it possible to lose so much time?

"You haven't been out the whole time, but it doesn't surprise me that you don't remember much. Now we're two peas in the same pod…at least memory-wise, I guess."

His attempts at humor didn't sit well. He'd said they were safe, but was that really true?

"Where are we?"

"Closer to the city than I'd like to be right now. A high school friend of mine's family uses this as a hunting lodge, but I'm pretty sure they haven't been here in more than a decade."

"You haven't…seen anyone?"

He shook his head. "Not yet. After I pulled you off the tree I hightailed it off the mountain. With your lung collapsed, I knew I'd never get it to reexpand at altitude, so I had to get you to lower ground. It seemed to work, but we're too close to civilization. We probably shouldn't stay here more than another day." He reached for a small oxygen monitor and placed it on her finger. "Your oxygen levels have been good over the last twelve hours."

Reaching to the floor again, he grabbed a stethoscope, another item she recognized from her father's kit.

He placed the bell against her chest. "You know what to do."

She took a deep breath and was immediately racked by a coughing fit. The tube sitting inside her chest had saved her life, but it also irritated her lung. She held her hand to her side, stabilizing the tube. It felt like a snake worming its way through her. Remnants of iodine remained on her skin. A shudder ran through her as she thought about what had lived on the tree branch as far as microorganisms and what might plume in her body if given enough time. She looked at the knots that held the tube in place.

It was not the standard tie generally taught to medical students. It was her father's special variety.

And Casper had used it.

He eased her back. The worry that clouded his eyes

seemed to be fading. She'd guessed he'd give the okay to stop digging her grave.

"I think we should see if you can tolerate eating anything. I ran out of IV fluids twelve hours ago, so if you're not able to drink we're going to have another problem on our hands."

He left her to go to the kitchen, which consisted of a small gas stove, a sink and little else. Next to the stove was a small countertop with a waiting mug. He poured hot water into it, grabbed a few other items and headed back in her direction.

"This time, you get the hot chocolate. Just try to sip it. You'll need the sugar. I'm guessing you feel pretty weak. Hopefully this will give you the boost that you need."

She reached for the mug. He was more on point than she cared to admit. She'd never been this incapacitated before...forced to rely on someone else for her basic needs. In a sense, it was unnerving, but Casper's thoughtfulness and care was filling a void in her. Her hands shook as she reached for the liquid, and Casper kept it steady as she sipped.

All it needed was a splash of peppermint and she'd feel like something was right with the world again.

After setting the cup on the floor, he handed her a few graham crackers with peanut butter—another favorite treat from her youth.

"Take it slow," he admonished her after she greedily polished the first cracker off. "There are no medications for nausea in your father's kit."

She nodded. He was right, but her stomach was celebrating. She didn't feel nauseated, just hungrier. The food was already making her feel better.

"Tell me what else you've remembered," Ashley said, taking smaller bites.

Casper busied himself for a few moments before answering. "A lot. Just not anything important that will help us right now."

"How do you know?" She nestled herself into the crook of the couch after finishing the second cracker. Casper gathered the blanket and tucked it around her body. The back of his hand came to rest on her forehead, lingering there longer than she felt necessary to measure a temperature, yet her body responded to his touch as if she were feverish.

He smiled. "Normal temperature. That's good. Hopefully I didn't give you a major infection."

"You're not answering my question. Perhaps something that seems insignificant to you and something that seems insignificant to me—together could be the clue as to what we're supposed to do next."

Reaching under the blanket, he pressed his fingers into her wrist to measure her pulse. He seemed to be doing everything he could not to answer her question or travel down his reestablished memories in order to help her. She grabbed his hand and pulled gently, coaxing him to look at her. "Casper, what are you afraid of?"

"Maybe I don't trust these memories and I don't want to make a decision based on something that might not be true that will put us in more danger."

"It seems to me like not talking about this, living in ignorant bliss as they say, will do us more harm than good," Ashley pressed.

Casper settled his elbows on his knees and rested his chin on his hands. "Do you remember me at all? Ever remember us meeting before?" he asked her.

The locked gaze in his eyes was almost dizzying, as if that look tried to pull forth some shared memory between the two of them.

Her father had been known to bring a lot of people by the house. He was an extrovert, constantly needing to be surrounded by people. The energy from those gatherings renewed his strength. Ashley had found herself reacting quite differently. She wasn't a wallflower by any means, but she needed solitude to get her bearings. Perhaps it was working in the ER, dealing with the range of mild accidents to horrible tragedies that caused her to be somewhat reclusive in her time off. Thinking back through some of these events that her father had insisted she suffer through, she couldn't recall Casper being any part of them.

"It was Christmas, maybe five years ago. You were just beginning your ER fellowship."

She rested her head back and closed her eyes. There had been so many of those parties that they all ran together in her mind. "I'm sorry. I don't, but don't take it personally."

His eyes softened. "Easy for you to say."

Was her comment some kind of sucker punch to his ego? Was he disappointed because maybe he'd been crushing on her in the past?

"All those parties may have gotten annoying to you, but for me, they were something I'd never experienced before. My family…just wasn't into celebrating."

"I'm sorry."

"It's just what it was. Families are different. Mine was more reserved. I guess I wanted something different—something more adventurous. Your father brought that out in me."

"I did like doing the white elephant gift exchange. It was always funny to see that what someone considered trash could be another person's treasure."

"Did you know your father was working for the CIA?" Casper asked.

The question jolted Ashley. A chill ran through her body. How could that even be possible? He was a doctor, not a spy.

"That was a joke, right?" Ashley asked.

"You never wondered why he traveled so much? Most doctors stay pretty close to home."

"We, as in my brother and my mom, thought it was mission work."

"I guess it was in a way…mission work. However, a lot more dangerous than offering help in clinics in developing countries."

"Depends on what area of the world you're in. The Ebola outbreak in Liberia was pretty dicey."

"Your father admitted to you he was there?" Casper asked.

"One of the few times he did. He was gone for almost six months."

Casper nodded, his lips pressed.

"What is it you're not telling me?"

Casper shrugged. "I'm pretty sure Jared Fleming was his handler."

Ashley's mouth gaped open.

"Like I said, I don't fully trust what I'm remembering. Let's just give it some time. More to drink?" he asked, holding up the cup.

Considering Casper's revelations about her father and Jared, she'd lost her ravenous appetite with those few words.

"And you?" she asked, waving the cup he offered away, almost not wanting to ask the question. "Did you work together in the CIA?"

Casper's eyes glanced away. He sat still for a few minutes. His silence was verification enough in her eyes. Finally, he turned back to her. "Yes, Russell recruited me, right after I finished my infectious disease fellowship."

Suddenly, her throat was dry and all she wanted was the cup of fluid back.

Right now, all this was turning out to be more than Ashley could take. Not only had her father been distant, but he'd also lied to her. The betrayal tarnished the precious few good memories she had of him. Maybe she was being selfish, but what little girl wasn't eager to have every spare ounce of her father's attention? To be the center of his world?

"If I told you he loved you...very much...you'd probably have a hard time believing that."

"You'd be right."

"I think these packages he sent you were more than just sharing information. It meant he trusted you. He knew you'd make the right decision with the information. Let me ask you...did your father ever give you other gifts from his 'travels'?"

"Sure. He always had presents when he came home for me and my brother."

"Anything that struck you as odd or unusual? Mysterious?"

"One time he brought me back a set of those Russian Matryoshka nesting dolls. It's one of my favorite toy gifts."

"You know, he gave me a set of those, as well. I found it kind of odd." Casper left her side and grabbed the pile of photos her father sent. "I've been analyzing these pictures a lot to see if anything struck me." He leafed through them until he found what he was looking for. "Was it like this one?"

Ashley narrowed her eyes. Her throat felt thick. Why

hadn't she noticed this before? Memories were a funny thing and perhaps Casper was right to be concerned because the person holding out that doll to her with outstretched arms was not her father, but a Russian scientist her father had brought to her house once to visit.

"I was at this party," Casper said.

"Vladimir was his name."

"He was a defector. One of the top Russian scientists during the heyday of their program, which they claim they've dismantled."

"My father said he was the head of a pharmaceutical company."

"That's one of the ways they disguised their activities... by framing them within the context of legitimate enterprises. Do you know what happened to him?"

"I don't think my father ever told me."

Casper tapped the stack of images against his other hand. "Do you know who else is in these photographs? Heads of Homeland Security, the NSA and the FBI. Some are former employees, but they still could have fingers within their organizations. I'm not calling them guilty, but it adds to my theory that your father didn't know who to trust."

Ashley's mind reeled. What exactly had her father been involved in?

"The point I wanted to make was that all of those things your father gave you were a way to stay connected to you. Some men use gifts as a substitute for emotional connection." His eyes grew distant for a moment. "His absence also safeguarded you against some evil men. I think, ultimately, he was trying to protect you."

Ashley's eyes teared. Had she been too harsh with her father growing up? Now all she wanted was to have him back.

"Where do we go next?"

Casper pointed to Vladimir again. "I know this man was convinced that the Russians were continuing their weapons program. He spent a lot of time trying to convince us, as in the US, not to let our guard down in respect to what our adversaries could create to kill us."

"How could Vladimir know for sure what the Russians were doing if he'd left the country?"

"Other than the fact that he taught them all the tricks that they know?" Casper sighed. Did he truly want to share this information with her? "Vladimir was convinced his old counterparts were trying to combine Ebola and smallpox."

"Why?"

"They wanted to have an unstoppable weapon. In his book, Vladimir wrote that he'd seen a successful test in rabbits. When the animals were infected they exhibited both signs of smallpox and Ebola."

"There's no cure for such a weapon, is there?" Ashley said.

"Exactly. This is always the main goal of any bioweapon. You don't want your enemy to have any chance of recovery."

A crushing weight settled over Ashley. All this new information…about her father…about the world…made her head spin. She didn't know what to do. What advice could she give Casper—a confessed spy?

"Who planted and detonated that device at the cabin?" Ashley asked. It was a question that had been burning in her mind. "Did putting the thumb drive into the computer trip it?"

"I don't know. I've been trying to figure that out, but it seemed like a trap for your father or whoever might come looking for him."

"What are we supposed to do? We can't investigate anything further while I have this tube in my chest and we don't know where to go." The light shifted in the cabin. Darkness was coming and the setting sun seemed representative of something other than just the time changing. What could they do?

"I'm aware of a safe house not too far from here. We'll go there tomorrow. The computer equipment should be secure and hopefully we'll be able to see what's on the thumb drive your father sent you."

Ashley turned on her left side away from Casper, her tears falling, and she didn't possess the energy required to wipe them away.

"Get some sleep. It's hard to see past the obstacles when you're tired."

She closed her eyes—more because she didn't want to continue this conversation with him. How could he be so positive considering their circumstances? Ashley dreaded tomorrow. Taking a chest tube out was not her idea of fun. And then what…more road travel? Every muscle in her body cried for rest…and not just for a few hours.

If only she could just go home.

NINE

Casper held on to Ashley's arm as she walked gingerly to the car, her hand pressing against her side where he'd removed the chest tube just a few hours ago. She was trying to be brave about it. What he wouldn't give to be able to administer to her something more potent than just the over-the-counter pain relievers, which she had taken both types of. Tears still welled in her eyes and the sharp, sympathetic pains in his own chest intensified with every tear that rolled down her cheek.

"Are you sure you're okay? How's your breathing?" Casper asked.

They were at their car and he opened the passenger door for her. Gingerly, she sat down, closed her eyes and pressed her head into the seat. Counterpressure was a known relief of pain. Did she also have a headache? The chest pain would be bad enough to deal with.

He kneeled on the ground next to her. "Ashley, I'll worry more if you don't say anything to me."

Ashley brushed the tears from her cheeks. "I'm fine, but I'm not fine." They both looked rough even though they'd taken somewhat warm baths. Casper had heated pots full of water on the woodstove to get something tolerable temperature-wise to bathe in.

"This whole thing is insanity," Ashley said. "I'm not even sure what we're trying to accomplish anymore. I was impaled by a tree branch—that's the kind of thing that can kill a person. You rigged up a chest tube. I've haven't even had a chest X-ray to know if my lung is inflated enough to be physically able to run from these people."

Casper both knew and didn't know what to say. Understanding the stress they were under was one thing but rationalizing it, explaining it, was another. Ashley was used to controlling uncontrollable things. It was her gift...her specialty. She'd had years of training perfecting it. Now their lives were anything but controllable. There were too many outside forces. Too many unknown questions. Both of them were broken mentally, physically...spiritually?

Part of her reaching the end of her emotional rope, he was sure, had to do with her lack of sleep. She'd tossed and turned through much of the night and he'd sat like a hawk, making sure the mason jar didn't spill over. If she'd been in a hospital, the end of her chest tube would have been in a much more secure contraption. Every time she'd moved he'd worried she would knock it over. With each toss and turn, he'd had to check to make sure everything was as it should be. Plus, sleeping on a dirty wooden floor didn't generally lull people into a deep sleep.

"We're both tired. I'm not sure what you want me to say. How can I help you? Physically, I'm confident your lung is fine. Your breathing is normal. Oxygen levels are good. You have pain, but it's to be expected. Remember, people lived through injuries much worse than yours without all the fancy medical equipment we have nowadays."

"True, but a lot of them died, too."

What could he say? She was right. Attempt number

one at reassuring a female had been an epic fail. Then again, with the amount of his memory that had returned, it was now clear he hadn't had a lot of relationships with women to practice such techniques.

Casper sat down on the ground next to her open car door and took a stick, pushing over rocks and leaves as he thought of the next thing to say. Each day seemed to give him a few more years of his memory back. Now, he remembered working with Ashley's father in the CIA hunting down bioweapons, taking care of people during outbreaks, but mostly keeping their eye out for others stealing the pathogens that infected their patients. After a virus infected its host, it generally mutated into something more potent. That was what every illegal bioweapons program wanted and foreign entities would send scavengers to collect it. Getting the mutation often required getting a sample directly from the source.

"We could go to the police, but I don't think that's a wise move. I think the number of these men within the CIA and other agencies that your father didn't trust is small—after all, most people working for these organizations are hardworking and respectable. The problem is we don't know how far the reach of these men is. Who they corrupted."

He gave her a chance to say something…anything. She remained silent, staring straight ahead.

"What we have to do is operate on facts that we know. We know that someone your father told you not to trust is looking for me. It could be that he knows about the packages. We know they'll kill to get their hands on what they want. We know it has something to do with bioweapons. Trying to tell a story like this to a local police department is going to get us psychiatric evaluations."

He waited as she processed his theory.

"I just feel lost. I want my life back…even with all its imperfections."

"I think the only possible way of making that happen is to take the next step. We have to follow the bit of information that your father gave you, which means finding out what is on that thumb drive. Maybe by the time we get to the safe house, I'll have remembered more and maybe know a person or two we can trust within the CIA. Until then, I think it's best to operate on our own."

She acquiesced, but Casper could tell it was with a healthy dose of reservation.

So be it.

He stood up, brushed the dead matter from his backside and got into the driver's seat. Ashley moved in stilted motions but was able to secure her own seat belt. It was what he wanted to see—that she was somewhat engaged in the process. Even though she doubted that this plan was the best course of action, she would try to do what she could to make the plan succeed.

Casper eased the car onto the road. He wanted to talk more, but all she did was lean against the door, her eyes distant and away from his own.

After hours of travel, they stopped at a gas station. Luckily, Casper had found some cash in her father's cabin that he'd stashed in the car before the explosion. They couldn't stay off the grid indefinitely, but hopefully it was enough to last them until they found the answers that they needed.

Ashley was in the bathroom attempting to freshen up. What she needed was a long hot bath. Something with bubbles sounded so luxurious her pulse quickened at the thought.

Her side ached, but it was tolerable. With each passing

mile, the chances of her lung deflating became more remote, but it hovered in the back of her mind as a risk and
it made her doubtful about being able to do any strenu-
ous activity.

At the sink, as she was rinsing her face with water,
she heard the faint squeak of door hinges. She groped for
a paper towel, patting the coarse fibers against her face.

When she glanced up into the fractured mirror there
was a man standing behind her.

Ashley turned to face him, her heart in her throat. The
paper towel she held drifted to the floor in surrender.

Jared Fleming.

How had he found them? He advanced forward two
steps. Instinctively, she backed up until the edge of the
porcelain bit into her back. She was pinned between this
dilapidated sink and the exit. He was simply dressed—
jeans and a red polo shirt. Chasing innocent people was
evidently easier in casual clothes.

He slid his fingers up her arm and cupped her chin
gently between his thumb and index finger. Ashley tensed
her body to keep him from sensing her trembling, but it
only intensified her shaking.

"I see that you weren't very honest with me. Here you
had Casper all along. Then I find out that you're Russell's daughter after you take Casper from the hospital
and that Russell may have sent something to you. Several items in fact. Your coworkers like to talk all about
your mysterious packages. When a doctor goes missing
with a patient, they feel it's their duty to spill all that they
know. Good, innocent people tend to do that."

Ashley swallowed hard. She tried to edge her head
back to free herself from his grip, but he only tightened
his fingers in response. How could his bony appendages
feel so much like steel?

"Did you know your father hid your true identity from me? Got fake pictures for his desk and everything." His teeth scraped over his lower lip. "Where are the items your father sent you?"

"I don't have them." That was the truth. They weren't physically on her body. Where was Casper? Was he still alive?

"Then you're going to show me where they are."

It was as if her body had a mind of its own. She shook her head almost imperceptivity, but it was like the pin being pulled from the grenade, releasing Jared's anger. He backhanded her so quickly she hadn't even seen his hand coming toward her face. First, she was falling. Then the blinding pain. Her teeth rattled. She reached out to catch herself, but he grabbed her shoulder and righted her before she splayed out at his feet. The pain in her chest flared.

Ashley brought her fingers up to her face. The remnants of his hand making contact with her cheek burned like acid. Tears welled in her eyes. She willed Casper to come to her. Had they done something to him? Or was he absent because she hadn't yet crossed that time frame where he'd be concerned about her missing.

The room spun. She blinked her eyes, hoping she was seeing what she thought and not manufacturing a hallucination due to a brain injury.

The door to the bathroom was cracked open…and widening.

She saw a hand grip the edge, pushing it open ever so slowly to prevent any noise from alerting the madman standing in front of her.

"Did you kill my father?"

Jared shrugged, like her question was something as insignificant as asking him for the time.

"What did he ever do to you? He trusted you. You were supposed to take care of him."

Jared released his grip from her shoulder and Ashley tilted off balance. Though it pained her to admit it, she'd been relying on his grip to keep her upright. She braced herself against the sink. Casper was now fully in the bathroom, having squeezed his body through the smallest crack, easing the door closed behind him.

"I did take care of him!" Jared yelled. "I gave him the world for his knowledge. He had everything he wanted until his moral compass reengaged. You—" he inhaled sharply "—and your family are going to lose everything now for the decisions he's made."

"For what?" Ashley asked. "What were these choices?"

"I'm not going to argue this point with you. The only thing I need from you is whatever your father sent you. Then you'll be coming with me."

Casper held a bat in his hands. Ashley tried not to betray his position with a glance of her eyes. If she stared at Jared directly, she could make out Casper's movements in the periphery.

"If you want to see your family again, you will give me those items."

Casper raised the bat above his head. He mouthed one word three times.

Duck!

Ashley dropped. The bat making contact with the side of Jared's body caused her stomach to flip with nausea. Jared groaned, falling first against the sink and then smacking his head on the dirty tile floor, landing over her and forcing her fully to the ground.

Casper quickly pulled the now unconscious Jared off her and grabbed her, pulling her up onto her feet. They ran back to the car and got in. Casper turned the engine over and drove his foot into the gas pedal. The car shot forward, even a little quicker than Casper expected, and the car shimmied violently side to side until he was able get purchase on the wheel.

"I don't know how long we have before they tail us. Somehow, they're tracking us. We need to figure out right now how. Are you okay? Did he hurt you?"

The adrenaline rush of what he'd done for her had muted the sting from Jared's slap. "Nothing I won't recover from. The tree was a little more vicious."

Casper nodded. "What did Jared say?"

Ashley turned around and looked behind them. Nothing but empty road. "He wants the things my father sent me. Was he alone?"

"No, with two others. That's what took me so long to get to you. I had to take care of them first."

"'Take care' as in keep them from following us or 'take care' as in they are no longer alive?"

Casper smoothed his fingers over his mouth. "No one's dead, although that would make our lives a lot easier."

Ashley settled forward. She'd asked Casper to get her a soda and some snacks from the gas station and they sat next to her in the cup holder. She grabbed the soda, drank and then reached for the package of peanut butter crackers. "Jared gave my father a lot of money and now he's mad because my father has changed his mind about something. He feels betrayed. He said my father found his moral compass again."

Casper drummed his fingers against the steering wheel. "When the Soviet Union collapsed, many of those scientists were offered obscene amounts of money for their expertise. Your father's knowledge base would be just as valuable."

Is that what happened around the time of my surgery

that fixed everything? My father accepted money from Jared to get us out of debt? What did he have to do for the money? Create a bioweapon?

Casper's voice pulled her back from her thoughts. "I can't tell you how invested the Russians were in making these weapons. When these men realized, right or wrong, the money they could be paid for sharing their knowledge, they became highly sought out by every foreign government bent on destruction."

"So the ones who were willing to share—"

"*Share* is too nice a word. *Sell* is more accurate."

"They quickly found work. And the others?"

"If they didn't comply and were captured, then they likely faced death."

Suddenly, the crackers Ashley had been snacking on didn't taste so good anymore. She set them aside.

"I'm not saying that's what happened to your father," Casper said quickly. "We don't know."

"My family was facing a financial crisis around the time of my heart surgery. Then…everything seemed better. This money my father took—what do you think he had to do in exchange?"

"If Jared has gone rogue and is paying agents on the side for work—then I'm afraid it probably isn't anything good."

"Do you think my father is still alive?"

Casper rested a hand on her arm and an overwhelming stillness filled the car. His touch was comforting, but was that all it meant? For the first time, she felt like she could trust a man to protect her. He'd already done so much to save her life, but something was shifting in her mind. Ashley was beginning to feel like she didn't want there to be a time when they weren't together. This sense of trust she had in him she'd never experienced before.

All her other relationships had been based on superficial physical attraction at best.

This trust…was deep, binding the two of them together. Was he beginning to feel this way, too? Is that what this touch meant? Or was it just a comforting gesture?

"I think we operate on what we know and we don't have any confirmation that he's dead. In fact, we have more evidence that he's alive…somewhere. The packages for one. If your father hasn't been sending them, then who?"

His words rang true. Maybe there would be an end to this awful nightmare. She fingered her necklace and worried it between her fingers.

The car swerved wildly to the right. "Where did you get that? That necklace? I didn't see you wearing it before."

"It was a gift from my father. It's usually in a case with the packages. All this talk about my father and our relationship—I just wanted to wear it today."

"Take it off," Casper ordered.

She clutched the charm in her fist. "No, it's one of the few things I have from him."

"It's got to be how they're tracking us."

"That's nonsense."

Casper pulled his hand away from her and clutched the wheel with both hands, his fingers taut under the pressure. He was angry with her.

"It's not nonsense. Tracking chips can be very small. If Jared has discovered the signal, he can follow it. Maybe your father gave it to you so he could keep tabs on you, maybe in case they took you, but now Jared knows it and he's using it against us. You have to get rid of it."

She turned away from him. What he asked was too

much. Ashley was sentimental about only a few things and this was one of them. She bit her lip to stave off more tears. Could he be right?

"I think something inside the jewelry case keeps it from being read. Probably has some kind of lining in it to keep it from transmitting when it's inside."

"Then what about the cabin? Why did it explode? How did they find us there? I wasn't wearing the necklace then."

"The computer must have been rigged somehow. They probably knew about the cabin and booby-trapped it, hoping to kill Russell in the process. The problem for Jared is the men working with him are probably few in number… they can't be everywhere. It's not an army we're against, just a few people. So they'll have to use some of these techniques to try to find us because, though it might seem like they are, they can't be everywhere at once."

She looked out the passenger window. Gray clouds gathered, mirroring the feeling of oppression that was beginning to overwhelm her. This necklace, to Casper, was just a thing that was aiding their enemy. To Ashley, it was one of the few items connected to a moment of real kinship with her father. It had been his gift to her on the day of her medical school graduation. One of the things he'd actually been present for.

"Ashley, please…"

She reached to the back of her neck with numb fingers and released the clasp. Before she could change her mind, she powered down her window and let it fall from her fingers.

TEN

This was the one place Casper remembered Russell telling him to go to—*if trust was an issue*. Those were the words that he'd added. He'd remembered the key code and they were able to get inside. The day had been a long one, and after Casper medically checked Ashley to ensure her lung was behaving itself, he tucked her into a bedroom with a dose of Tylenol and insisted she sleep.

Here they should be safe. They would be able to get the thumb drive into a computer without it tripping a baited trap. Ashley had been sullen most of the day... their conversation only at the barest minimum after she tossed the necklace out the window. Seemingly, getting rid of the jewelry had done the trick. They hadn't been followed. Daringly, they'd even stopped at a mom-and-pop sub shop for food and waited, almost tempting their captors to find them, and not a single person had entered the fast-food dive as they ate.

In the living room was a fireplace—this one easy to light. With the flick of a switch it was on. Casper sat on the couch, warm bottled water next to him. Ashley had refused to eat anything for dinner, which gnawed at his gut. However, he didn't feel like he could push her anymore. She was at her limit. She needed rest. A clear mind. They were still being hunted with no end to their predicament in sight.

Guilt washed over him. He'd wanted to tell Ashley something, but he couldn't bring the words from his lips. Saying them out loud, especially to someone else, would mean they could never be taken away. It would solidify them, and for most of the day he'd wrestled with whether or not what he'd remembered was actually true.

A small container of microwave mac and cheese sat next to the water untouched. He forced a bite into his mouth. One of them had to keep their strength up. Sad to say, but he was in better shape than Ashley, even as broken as he felt.

Because he remembered Ethan dying.

What was at stake now was more than just keeping the two of them alive. They'd had intelligence about a probable bioweapons attack. That was what he and Ethan had been trying to prevent and likely what Jared Fleming was trying to perpetuate.

Massive death.

But why? What would cause a patriot to turn against his own country? To unleash a deadly bioweapons attack against his own people? Casper knew he had to determine the answer to that question. If he could understand his enemy—his motivations—maybe deciphering the pieces that Ashley and he held would be the only thing to stop the coming wave.

Did Ethan's family know he was gone? Casper felt like it was his duty to tell them. What had happened to his body? He remembered their brutal assault getting interrupted by the burly man walking the dog. The zipping pain through his chest that had brought him back to life. His memory was clear, but there was still so much unknown.

He had to solve this. Had to make sure Ethan was remembered as a hero. That was the least he could do.

As he was forcing down bites of mac and cheese, Ashley emerged from the bedroom, a hand resting at her old chest tube site. He checked his watch. Maybe three hours had passed since he'd insisted she lie down. She smoothed her fingers through the tangles in her hair and sat next to him on the couch.

He lifted the empty cup. "Want me to whip you up some of this fabulous cuisine?"

"Later."

He wrapped an arm around her shoulders. It felt natural, despite the circumstances, the two of them sitting there. It was that comfortable quiet, where neither one felt forced to say anything.

"Why haven't you tried to sleep?" Ashley asked.

"I've been thinking about a lot of stuff."

"More memories?" Ashley asked.

"All of them." She stiffened slightly, and then relaxed. He waited for her questions, mildly surprised when she didn't press the point. "No interrogation?"

"I trust you to tell me what you think is important."

That seemed too easy. Did she trust him to that extent? "There's no burning question on your mind?"

"For the moment, I just want this. To feel calm… peaceful."

She wedged herself more into his side. "There's something funny about this safe house."

"What's that?"

"It's not an—how do I say this?—American safe house."

"No, it's not."

"Russian?"

"No, that would just be going into the other enemy camp. Ukrainian."

"I guess I never thought about other countries having safe houses here."

"Your father said to come here if I was ever lost and didn't know who to trust. Maybe he bought it from them. Maybe they lack the resources to keep it up."

"Makes me feel like an international fugitive," Ashley said. "There's a computer in the corner," Ashley noted.

"I see it," Casper said. "While you were resting, I did a pretty thorough search of the grounds and inside. I didn't see anything suspicious—no bombs waiting to explode. I get the sense someone has been here, though—in the last week or so. The items in the refrigerator aren't expired. There's fresh fruit in there."

"You trust this place enough to eat it?"

"The mac and cheese didn't kill me. It doesn't seem like anyone is living here. There are no clothes. The beds are made. The bathrooms look hotel ready. Almost like someone might have expected us to come here."

"Not an enemy?"

"Doubtful. It would make sense your father would develop a network of people he could trust outside the CIA. If you want to spoil a terrorist's plan, you have to have a network just like they do—a support network for undercover investigators."

"Is that what we are? The only hope to stop whatever this is?"

"I don't know, but we have to—"

"Let me guess…operate on facts."

"Exactly."

Casper pulled the thumb drive out of his pocket. He'd been holding on to it since Ashley got sick. He wanted to ask her about how she was feeling, but every time he had in the past twelve hours she'd given him an exacerbated look. There was a lot one could discern about a person's breathing without placing a stethoscope to their chests. Her breathing was relaxed, rhythmic. She could speak in full sentences without clipping her words between breaths.

Lord, thank You for giving me what I needed to save her life. Thank You for keeping us safe. Help us figure out what our next step is.

"Guess there's no time like the present to see what's on it," Casper said.

He opened his palm and she took the thumb drive from his hand.

There was more than one reason why Ashley wanted to see what was on the drive. Sitting so close to Casper had become a little unnerving. Her palms were still sweating and all she needed was him to try to check her pulse again and discover the emotions behind her nerves.

Never could she say that she'd fallen for a man before. Plenty of infatuations, but this felt different. Like Casper was stepping into a gap of unfulfilled need she'd had for a long time. Of companionship. Of trust. She couldn't deny her father's long absences over the years likely played into this and she didn't feel permanently scarred, but neither could she discount the impact it had had.

Ashley pressed the button to turn on the computer and waited for it to warm up. Casper pulled out the desk chair and motioned for her to sit down. The computer screen popped up. No skull of death laughing at them and dripping blood. She pushed the thumb drive in and held her breath. The machine whirred softly. Casper lowered his body so he could see the screen better, but the physical closeness caused her chest to vibrate. Could he sense that?

The computer signaled the drive had been installed. Ashley opened it and began to look through the files.

"Recognize any of these names?" Ashley asked.

Casper shook his head. "Might as well start opening them from the top."

Ashley clicked open the first file folder and noticed a series of pictures. She clicked on the first one, which opened the photo viewer, and she began to click through the series. There were more photos of her dad, some with Jared, some with the Russian scientist and US security intelligence.

She clicked through them quickly—stopping at one with her mother and Jared. They sat at a table and her mother looked…lovingly at Jared's face. That was the only way Ashley could describe it. Did that look mean anything? Whatever it was, Jared seemed oblivious. Perhaps it was nothing.

"Go to the next one. I don't know if any of those photos have new information for us. Those seem to be where he copied the pictures that he sent you in the packages."

She closed the photos and clicked on the next file down. What opened were scans of two small-town Colorado newspaper articles. One was dated last year. The other about six months ago.

"'Local Community Fears Smallpox Outbreak,'" Casper read out loud.

"I thought smallpox was considered eradicated," Ashley said.

"The last natural case was in 1977."

"*Natural* being the operative word," Ashley verified.

"Exactly."

Ashley scrolled through the contents. "This town isn't too far from where we're at. Maybe a three-hour drive."

Casper leaned in closer, his breath puffing against her neck.

"Maybe you should grab a chair," Ashley suggested.

Ashley pulled off the jacket she was wearing. How could she be physically attracted to a man right now, considering the state both of them were in? Casper wasn't thrilled with her taking a prolonged soak in a bathtub until the stitches in her side were out, but a long hot shower seemed in order. As he stepped away, she sniffed her shirt. It smelled. Not like smoke from the explosive cabin fire. Like the musty cabin had tainted it. Was the heat she felt a temperature or evidence of her attraction to Casper?

Ashley shifted her chair over to make room for him. Having him sit down next to her instead of hovering didn't abate her symptoms.

She grabbed his hand and placed the back of it against her forehead. "Does it feel like I have a fever?"

"You know this is the worst way to measure. It's not scientifically accurate."

"You didn't feel that way before. I don't agree with you and neither does every mother in America. Do I feel warm?"

He reached his hand up again and lightly touched her forehead, then her cheeks. "You feel fine. No fever."

His touch unnerved her. This was bordering on ridiculous. They were on the run...for their lives. How could she even be thinking about this?

Casper pointed to the screen. "This other town is relatively close, as well. They're perhaps a couple of hours apart."

Ashley read out loud. "'Local health officials are concerned about a group of patients that presented recently to a local community hospital with symptoms resembling smallpox. "It's not clear what illness they have," one anonymous source explained. "The medical picture is complicated. We believe more than one disease might be at play. Whatever it is, it's highly contagious." Four health-care workers who took care of the sickened patients also contracted the disease—as well as several townspeople. Local officials are working to contain the illness. It is unknown how the patients originally contracted the disease. If you have a fever accompanied by a rash, stay home and contact health officials at the following number."' Ashley slumped back in her chair. "Did you ever hear about this?"

"No, but I'm not surprised this didn't make headlines countrywide. There have been lots of outbreaks that haven't been covered by the national media. Notice how they didn't say the word *Ebola*? How they were trying to quarantine possible cases without calling it just that? It would have caused mass panic. Plus, if this is covert—it's not surprising more local media didn't catch wind of it."

Ashley swallowed hard. "Whatever this mysterious disease is, it struck in two instances, six months apart. It could be something naturally occurring, but I'm doubtful. It if exhibits the symptomology of two separate disease processes my guess is that it was engineered."

"Me, too. Perhaps you should have been an infectious disease doctor," Casper said.

"Do you know how nervous I get? I'm sort of a germophobe at heart."

"You don't think you're practicing in the wrong area then? You're our first line of defense for things like this—the first to be exposed. The canary in the coal mine for any sort of biomedical attack."

Ashley put her hand up to stop him. "You're not helping. I try not to think about it."

Casper laughed softly. "What's the next file?"

After several clicks, the file opened. It was a series of maps. One had five red circles.

Ashley tapped the screen. "Do you see this?"

Casper leaned closer. His cheek was inches from hers. Her heart skipped a few beats. What she needed was a glass of water. "Two of those circles are around the towns where the mysterious illness happened. Black Falls and Aspen Ridge. In the other three circles are numbers."

"They're all the number four. They sit in the middle of nowhere, but this one seems equidistant between the two towns."

"What could the number four mean?" Ashley asked.

"The only reference I can think of that might pertain to this situation is in relation to lab biosafety levels, as in what type of pathogens a lab can work with. Level four is the highest."

"Why would they be in the middle of nowhere?"

"For protection. It doesn't seem like we abide much by this now, but distance is a great precaution against spreading a disease you're tinkering with from a lab into a community. The Soviet Union learned that the hard way once with an accidental release of weapons-grade anthrax because a lab worker noted a broken filter needed repair on a Post-it note, not through the proper channels, and no one figured it out until hours later. In that time, countless spores were released. Most night shift workers at a plant across the street died from inhaled anthrax. No distance to protect them."

"Okay, I see your point, but what that also tells me is that the infections in those two towns, if we believe that whatever infected those people was engineered, could have been intentional because they are so far away from the labs. They don't sit across the street. They are miles away."

Casper nodded. "You could be right. If these outbreaks were intentionally released it proves my point about people living far away from an experimental lab as protective. Things can be carried on the wind for long distances, though. It would make rodent transmission doubtful. If you infected a few rats and just let them go…it's a long way for them to travel."

"How do you think the people in the two different towns were infected?" Ashley asked.

"I have no idea. If this pathogen is a new creation, then I wouldn't have any knowledge base on transmission and we don't know what the health care workers were wearing to protect themselves. The best way to find out is to go to one of these towns and start snooping around."

"Why not go to the lab first?"

"Might be helpful to know exactly what we might be getting ourselves into…what kind of pathogens we might be exposed to. In the towns, the pathogen has likely burned itself out. I mean, Miss Germophobe, if you want to run right into an unknown lab without any biohazard gear then—"

"Okay, I see your point. Town investigation first."

She opened the next series of files. The information she was seeing didn't make any sense to her.

Casper moaned and slouched in his chair.

Clearly, he didn't like what he saw.

ELEVEN

Casper's throat was closing off from the dread invoked by the image on the computer screen. Someone had done it…really done it. Created the most lethal…most virulent bioweapon known to man. His body leached cold sweat, and he longed for the warm blankets Ashley had once given him at the hospital.

"Casper, what is it? You don't look well."

He didn't feel well. His stomach roiled, killing his hunger, as his body released a flood of acidic bile. It crept up his throat. Something like this was every infectious disease doctor's worst nightmare.

Coming across a pathogen that could not be killed and yet could kill so many.

"It's a microscopic image of a pathogen," Casper said, his voice cracked with emotion. He'd thought he'd remembered everything, but seeing this photograph brought back dreaded memories. His amnesia had caused him to forget his time in Liberia, but now that his memory was mostly back, his psyche was likely protecting him from easily recalling the trauma he suffered.

"What is it?" Ashley asked, her voice soft, sullen.

"Have you ever seen anyone die of Ebola?"

She merely shook her head, her eyes wide, as if she

fed off his fear without him having using the words thus far to express the horror his body felt.

"When outbreaks happen, there's a good chance the pathogen will mutate into something different...oftentimes something more virulent. The host's immune system is a challenge, an obstacle for the pathogen to overcome. If it does, it's usually stronger, and much harder to kill."

How true that is even of us as humans. When we go through life's difficulties—we are often stronger on the other side. Who could blame a virus for doing the same thing?

"Were you helping patients?" Ashley asked.

"For a while, Russell and I just sat back and observed, but the local organization helping during the crisis was overwhelmed and so I offered my services for a few weeks. It was a risk, but I felt like I would also have an easier time telling if someone was trying to steal samples."

"Because if the pathogen mutated it could make a better weapon."

"Exactly," Casper said. He pointed back to the computer screen. "You asked me which pathogen this was. This is actually the combination of two different pathogens. Ebola and smallpox."

"How is that possible?"

"In those series of photos are pictures of Russian scientists who left the Soviet Union after its collapse. I told you how poorly they were paid for their work and how valuable they were on the open market. Some, like Vladimir, who wrote the book, are using their knowledge to prevent such attacks. Others were probably tempted by the money. You'd have to be. I'm sure it was more than they'd ever thought they'd see in their lifetimes."

Casper eased the mouse from Ashley's fingers and

went back to the photos. He clicked to the one that showed three strangers, her father and Jared Fleming. "This is Vladimir. These two other men were underlings of his, so they certainly had his knowledge base. From these photos, we know Jared was at least introduced to them at one point. He could have hired them, or brokered them out to another entity for a fee."

"You don't think the US is doing this?"

"No, but it doesn't mean it's not happening on US soil. It probably would be hard to convince these men to go back to Russia after the freedom they experienced here."

He clicked back to the files and opened up the next one.

The world definitely looked dimmer.

"What is this? It looks like a recipe, except there are hundreds of pages."

"It is," Casper said, wiping cold sweat from his brow. "For weapons-grade ES1. Remember those codes you found in your father's cabin—ES1 is the code for this bioweapon. This is the cookbook for how to manufacture it. This is straight from the Soviet playbook. It's more evidence that a bioweapons attack using this pathogen is more than feasible…likely probable. Entities that use a system like this don't create these formulations until they have a proven product on their hands."

"What are the last two files?" Ashley asked.

Casper tried to open them. They were password protected. He tried a few variations. Ashley's name. His name. Both their names. Birth dates. He shoved the keyboard back in exacerbation. Another piece of the puzzle locked down. What could Ashley's father be protecting? If this thumb drive fell into the enemy's hands—what would Russell not want them to find? The answer to the password would likely have to be deciphered from what Russell had sent Ashley.

Tears fell silently down Ashley's face. Suddenly, she stood up and began to back away from the computer. A response to Casper's smoldering anger?

He stood up and grasped for her, grabbing her shirttail just as she was almost out of reach. She stopped. Taking two steps closer to her, he turned her around. She buried her face in her hands and all he could think to do was draw her into a tight embrace. He smoothed his hand over her hair until the shuddering from her body eased.

"What is it?" he asked softly.

It seemed like endless minutes before she could form a sentence to respond to his inquiry.

"Do you…think my father…made this…?"

Weapon.

That was the word she left out. How must it be for a daughter, a healer, to learn dark, secretive things about a father who hadn't really been straight with her? And even though his memories were clearer, he hadn't really shared with Ashley what he had come to understand about his mentor…that he'd even been a mentor to Casper.

"No. I just can't see it."

Ashley pulled away. Her sapphire-blue eyes implored his for truth. "How can you be so sure?"

"Because the man I know *would never* do this. His whole life was spent exposing people who created these abominations to keep the world safe. To keep you safe."

"Me? Of course, every man wants his family safe."

"No, they don't. Most…sure, but the creators of ES1 can't possibly believe in the sanctify of life when they've invented something that could destroy us all. I know your father… I know he could never do that."

"The man you speak of feels like a stranger to me."

"His distance, though hard for you I'm sure, was meant for your safety. It would break him to hear you say these things. He talked about you often and always with pride. You and your brother both."

"Then where is he?"

Casper slid his hand down her arm. "I don't know, but I think what he's hiding is threatening the livelihood of criminal men and that's dangerous." He brought his thumbs up to her cheeks. "I feel like I know so much about you from his stories. A man doesn't share things like that out of disinterest."

Ashley placed her hands over his. "Like what?"

"He shared…everything. Your college graduation. How proud he was when you went into medicine. Childhood stories about what a tomboy you were."

She looked at him. A longing in her eyes drew him half a step closer. He didn't want to confuse this moment. Was this look just a pleading for more information about her father or was it a signal in response to how he was feeling about her? A signal that she thought he was worth taking a risk for.

"Clearly, I grew out of that phase," she whispered.

"You're beautiful."

Her eyes widened in surprise. She inched closer to him. His heart rocketed into his throat as she placed one of her hands against his neck, stepping a little bit closer. "You can kiss me, if you want to."

His mind reeled. Tentatively, he pulled her toward him, his lips soft against hers. She eased into him and his hands slid around her back to hold her tight. He felt light-headed from the rush. She eased back and he reluctantly let her drift away.

She smiled. "I was worried you wouldn't take me up on my offer."

He laughed and reached for her hand. "I just hope that won't be our last. I—" he gripped her hand tighter "—want to know everything about you…from you… not your father. I mean, I don't know many women who could survive getting impaled on a tree."

"What do we do next?" Ashley asked.

"Tomorrow we'll go to ground zero."

"Ground zero for what?"

"The first breakout of ES1. Black Falls, Colorado."

Ashley could hardly sleep. The warmth she'd felt from Casper's kiss stuck with her. What was this thing? She'd never been so bold before. Yes, she'd been smitten by men, but there was something about Casper that was different. He was genuine. Authentic. Men she met and dated were mostly infatuated by her looks and her job, but Casper connected with her on an entirely different level.

Plus, considering this crisis they were in, he was as calm as any of her seasoned coworkers. She felt safe being with him. Wanted to be close to him. Was this how love started? Casper didn't weigh every permutation of a situation in his mind, whereas an ER physician was trained to consider every possibility no matter how remote. Casper liked to operate only with the present facts while she liked to consider all facets of a situation. Together, these differences made them strong. He could reel her back in if she got too off track and she could make him examine a problem from a different angle.

They always said that opposites attract.

What Casper said about her father made her look at him in a different light. He knew him on a deeper level than she did. Perhaps they'd developed such a kinship because her father knew Casper was a person he could trust and so he was more open with him about his feel-ings. Maybe her father wasn't the closed-off stone of ice she'd made him out to be in her mind.

That his distance—what she considered standoffishness—was a border of protection around her family.

Something she should be thankful for considering the kind of work he was involved in.

Will I ever get the chance to see my father again? To see if these things that Casper believes about him are really true?

Ashley turned to her other side. Something bothered her about the files. If what Casper said was true, that perhaps the files were password encrypted to protect the information from falling into enemy hands, then perhaps it wasn't something bad, but something good. Casper had mentioned that these thugs always tried to have their Frankenstein-like pathogens be able to overcome a cure.

What if those protected files contained the cure?

Then the password would have to be something that only a trusted person would know. Maybe something only she would know. Nothing that could be discovered from the packages her father sent because what if those, or any part of their contents, were intercepted?

The password couldn't be exclusive just to her because what if something happened to her and she was unable to provide the password?

Seemingly, her father wanted her and Casper together. Many clues to the puzzle were solved because of information they had shared with one another. Where had she and Casper first met?

The Christmas party? The doll had been a gift. It had been unusual to say the least. Memorable.

For both of them.

Ashley threw the covers aside, exited her room and ran headlong into Casper as he exited his. Both of them tumbled to the ground in a knot of arms and legs. Ashley scrambled to her feet, her heart racing—initially she'd thought she'd run straight into an intruder.

"Casper! What are you doing out here? I think my heart stopped." Ashley pressed her hand into her chest.

He took a few steps back, a look of amusement on his face. "I should ask you the same thing."

"The password. I think I might know what it is."

"Me, too," he said.

"What do you think it is?" Ashley said.

He crossed his arms over his chest. "Matryoshka."

She nodded and they both raced to the computer. When the blank field popped up, she typed in the word.

The file opened.

Ashley scanned through pages. "Do you know what this is?"

"Another recipe."

"Great, just what we need. Another pathogen to worry about," Ashley said, straightening up.

"No, you're wrong. I think this is the cure."

TWELVE

The town of Black Falls, Colorado, was aptly named.

It was a ghost town, and in the distance, Casper could see a waterfall tumbling over rocks that looked smudged with coal dust. He parked in front of a boarded-up diner that had enough large holes running through the side of the building that the plywood covering the front door seemed foolish. They exited the car and stood, examining the landscape around them.

"What do you think happened here?" Ashley asked.

"Looks like we'll need to do some digging to find out."

"In there?"

"Can you think of a better place? The town's not that big and the location of the medical center isn't clearly obvious. It could be miles from here. Maybe there's a phone book in there or something. An old newspaper. Probably should look in each of these structures."

"After you." Ashley motioned.

"No, ladies first." Casper smiled.

"Not when there're snakes and other undesirable creepy crawlies inside. I've already faced one life-threatening event."

Ashley didn't turn to him as she said those words. She probably meant it as a joke, but her tone suggested otherwise. Maybe humor in light of what they were seeing wasn't appropriate. Her mood seemed dampened, wary.

Even the sky seemed angry as it brewed new storm clouds.

He stepped up to the crumbling sidewalk. A few steps to the side of the door, he was able to duck down and enter the diner. Life here looked suspended. There were still dirty plates and glasses on the tables. Food that may have remained had likely been scavenged by the varmints Ashley feared.

Evidently, even ER doctors had their limits.

He went behind the service counter, the red tile broken. Looked like the copper piping had been taken. He shuffled around until he found what he hoped for.

An old stack of town newspapers of varying dates spanning a two-month period. It looked like the paper was generated once a week and so perhaps they could give him an indication of whether anything mysterious had happened that might correlate to the demise of the town. He set them on the counter, setting tufts of dirt into the air, and he wondered if there was anything biological attached to them.

Ashley had gone into the back kitchen area. Intermittently, there was metallic banging as pots dropped onto the floor. Glass ruptured.

"Are you okay?" Casper called to her.

"I think I found something interesting. I'll bring it to you."

Casper turned his attention back to the newspaper stack and flipped through the pages. A black four-door sedan drove down the street. Casper held his breath as it passed.

Keep going...keep going.

Another metal pot clanged to the floor. Casper hunched

his shoulders. He didn't see the car stop. He left the counter and stepped out onto the street.

The car continued. No brake lights.

His hackles rose. Should he grab Ashley and leave? The town was deserted but the road was maybe one of the few paved ones around. They needed to stay. They needed to find the next step.

Casper watched. The car continued until it was out of sight.

With raw nerves, he returned to the counter and the stack of news stories.

It didn't take long to find the first story pertaining to the mysterious illness. Three teens were out after curfew when they'd been entranced by two larger-than-normal red balloons floating toward town. They were hopeful for treasure of some kind as a nearby larger town often did such things during their annual balloon festivals—leaving raffle tickets inside to claim prizes with. The teens remarked on how the balloons looked different, and were smaller in number, and that it had still been early for the annual release. Also, the balloons the festival used were always white.

According to the story, they followed the objects until one popped, dropping an item from the sky not far from where they were standing. They described it as an oversize jingle bell.

Casper's blood ran cold. Never did he think he'd see anything like this on United States soil, but there it was, right in front of his face in black-and-white.

A whoosh of air tickled the back of his neck and Ashley popped through the door. The first thing Casper registered in his mind was the dirty yellow color—a caution signal erupted in his mind. She laid the suit on the counter and plopped a respirator on top of it.

An old biohazard suit. Casper noted the tears in the fabric—definitely wouldn't be functional now.

"There are three of these stored in the back." And then, ever so gently, she laid a grenade on top of the suit, as if to prevent its detonation by cushioning it on something soft.

The pin was still in place.

Casper's fingers tingled. "How many of those did you find?"

"Just the one," Ashley said. "But I stopped digging once I stumbled onto it."

Casper took it and placed it in the pocket of his jacket. *Why would there be grenades here? What could they have been used for? Who left all these things behind and why?*

Pushing the thoughts aside, he pointed to the picture he'd found in the newspaper. "This is a bomblet. It's used to deliver weapons-grade pathogens. The cracks release the contents."

"Like the video of the anthrax dispersal on Gruinard Island. A missile without any explosion—I hope I never experience anything like that."

"Exactly."

"Where was this one found?" Ashley asked.

"Here."

"This town?"

Casper nodded. Ashley leaned against the counter.

"Someone hit this town with a missile containing a bioweapon?" Ashley asked.

"No, not a missile. I think balloons."

Ashley stood up, eyeing him disbelievingly. "Now you're getting into fantasy. That's pure fiction."

Casper leaned his hip against the counter and crossed

his arms over his chest. "Yet, you found a collection of biohazard suits in the back of a diner."

Ashley smirked.

Casper placed a finger on the news article. "It's actually not that far-fetched. During World War II, Japan was also interested in the use of biological weapons. Their facility was called Unit 731. There is documentation of a planned attack on the US code-named Cherry Blossoms at Night, and a permutation of that plan was to have balloons carry the agent to the Western US."

Absentmindedly, Ashley smoothed her hand over the suit. Casper prayed nothing residual remained on it, like anthrax spores.

"Maybe you shouldn't touch that anymore," Casper said.

She yanked her hand away, brushing them quickly against one another. Even though the action likely made her feel better mentally, it would do little to keep from getting contaminated. In fact, if it was something like anthrax, she was kicking spores into the air.

He placed his hands over hers. "It's okay. You're probably fine. Just keep your hands down. Don't touch your face or anything."

She sighed but relented. "Maybe you should pass me some of those papers. Let me help you sort through them to see if we can find anything else."

He did as she asked. He kept the first month and handed her the rest. Casper flipped through his pages more quickly. Something was causing the hair on his arms to stand on end. It didn't take him long to find what he was looking for. His heartbeat ticked up a notch. He nudged Ashley's side with his elbow, laid the paper out in front of her and pointed to the article. It appeared in the third week of the first month.

"'Mysterious Illness Infects Three Local Teens,'" Ashley read.

"The story is a couple of weeks after they found the bomblet."

"What were their symptoms?"

"It doesn't specify anything other than a flu-like illness. At this reporting, one of them had already died. It lists the name of the hospital—Black Falls Medical Center."

Casper continued onto the next edition. "Just found notices of death for all three teens."

Ashley gasped as she unfolded one of her papers. "Black Falls Medical Center Closed after Fire Related to Gas Leak."

Definitely suspicious. "When did that happen?"

"Let me see the date on the paper that had the obituaries."

Casper slid his paper over and Ashley compared the two dates. "Looks like shortly after the boys' deaths. Hard to figure out an exact timeline. Could have been just days."

"The hospital closing could explain the demise of this town. Even a small hospital was likely this place's largest employer. That's our next stop."

"Did you see the old pay phone over there? I think there's still a yellow pages tucked in the shelf underneath." She left him and came back within a few minutes, the dust-covered relic in her hands.

She flipped it open. "Found it. An address for the hospital."

Casper looked around the diner. There was a turnstile rack that held maps. He went to it and pulled one out that seemed to highlight the area.

Another clang of pots came from the back of the diner.

Casper's nerves fired. Ashley and Casper locked eyes. Through the opening of the kitchen pass-through, he saw the flash of a man clad in black clothes raise a weapon. Casper ran to the counter, grabbed Ashley by the shoulders, pulled her over the top of it and to the ground on the other side. He covered her body with his just as the bullets went flying. Whatever glass had been intact shattered around in a violent storm of shards. The noise was deafening, and Casper's ears started to ring.

The bullets stopped. The clicking of new clips being loaded.

"Isn't it time the two of you gave up?"

Jared and his goons had found them. How?

Neither of them spoke in response to his question.

Casper should have trusted his gut upon seeing the car. They'd merely persuaded him that they'd left town in order to circle back and set up a sneak attack. Casper lifted his head, gritting his teeth to keep from coughing from the dust, and eyed the distance to their car.

No chance they would make it without getting shot from behind. He heard footsteps—the whine of the hinges of the double doors opening. The air charged with his apprehension. He reached into his pocket and grabbed the grenade.

He eased off Ashley and pushed her closer to the diner's counter. Before he could convince himself not to, he pulled the pin on the grenade, counted to two, stood, hurled the explosive through the kitchen pass-through and then shielded Ashley with his body.

The shock wave of the explosion shoved their bodies toward the front of the diner. The counter splintered open. Casper sat up and brushed debris from his face. Ashley was on her elbows, her face covered in a fine spray of dust.

Do I go check to see if Jared and his men are still alive or do we just run?

Casper stood, his legs shaky, and saw the wall behind the counter had ruptured open. A pile of rubble shifted indicating movement.

He held his hand out to Ashley. "We need to go... right now."

Within thirty minutes they arrived at Black Falls Medical Center, which seemed to be a glorified two-story clinic, half of it burned down. Had it truly been a gas leak? Or had a perfectly placed explosive caused the fire?

The sense of foreboding that overcame Ashley caused her blood to pour an icy wave through her body. She shuddered and pulled her jacket tighter around her body. The hospital sat at the top of a modest hill. The black pavement of the curving road was like a shed snakeskin—no longer perfect with its pocked holes and broken lines.

They'd parked off the road, hidden behind a fallen road sign, to see if they were being followed. Nothing moved for another ten minutes, and Casper seemingly deemed that it was safe enough to check out the facility.

"We can't stay here long. If Jared's alive, it won't take much for him to guess we'd come here."

Casper parked at the back entrance under the old ambulance bay. The cement block stopgaps were broken and rusted rebar poked through like singular broken teeth in an otherwise vacant gum line. They both got out of the car, but stood and looked at the structure countless minutes. Common sense was begging Ashley to run, but if they didn't figure out who they could entrust this information to then they would always be hunted because of what was on that drive. Even though it was risky, gathering this information, particularly if it involved Jared Fleming, could ensure their safety in the end.

And what was their working theory anyway? She and Casper hadn't really verbalized it to one another. Her father had a lot of information on a new bioweapon and a cure for it. Jared seemed interested in that information and Casper, and yet her father had told her never to trust Jared. Which meant, if her father was on the run from him, then any additional incriminating evidence about Jared could only help her father get his life back.

Casper's voice broke into her thoughts. "I think we need to look for evidence that could incriminate Jared."

"I was just thinking the same thing," Ashley said. "Even though much of your memory is back, you haven't shared much about him. Do you think these insinuations my dad always made about Jared are true?"

Casper eased the car door closed behind him. The wind rustled his hair gently. "I would trust your father over Jared. In all the time I was with your father, he never did anything that would make me question his honesty. He was tasked with exposing the bioweapons programs of other countries. He was very good at his work."

"Do you know of any motive that would explain why Jared would want to hurt my father?"

"Jared has had a lot of training in presenting everything but his authentic self. Who knows who the real Jared Fleming is and what his interests are? Part of the problem with being a spy is that you can lose yourself in these other identities you've created. You can begin to believe counterarguments against your government. You can get a lot of money for selling your secrets if you can finesse a deal before you're caught and killed for being a double agent."

"Do you find it strange that the cemetery is right over there?" Ashley pointed to her right.

"Few things surprise me anymore. Shall we venture in?"

Ashley's hands cooled. "You think it's safe?"

"It's stood this long so probably. But also safer than what we've already been through."

The glass to the sliding ambulance doors into the ER were broken and so they merely walked through it. It wasn't simply that the floor was dirty. It was as if a tsunami of dust had rolled in and erased what had been present before. As they walked, the filth was deep enough that it felt like they were walking on a beach. The first sign they came to pointed to the right for the medical records department.

The very direction of the burned-out portion of the structure. Nervous waves poured through Ashley's body. Mice scampered about visibly, unafraid. She gritted her teeth so she wouldn't scream.

"Interesting, right?" Ashley asked.

"That the medical records department is likely gone? A little too convenient for my tastes."

"If the explosion happened shortly after these boys died, it's possible their records wouldn't be there. They could still be on the floor. Depends on how organized the records department was."

Casper took a few steps away from the wall. There was an elevator to their left. "Door to the staircase is right here. Hopefully they'll be sturdy enough to hold us."

They weren't as crumbled as the road that led them here. It took three good tries before the rusty hinges allowed Casper to shoulder through the door. The medical unit was an open room. Remnants of curtains hung from the ceiling and a few beds, though knocked over, remained. What Ashley guessed was the nurses' station was located at one end of the room. A turnstile held the characteristic plastic folders that used to house patient charts. Now everything was moving toward electronic records, but the transition had been hard for smaller hospitals to undertake.

Ashley walked to the counter and pulled the first chart. She pointed to the top and it listed one of the teen's names on the end. Her breath quickened. When she popped up the front cover, there were no papers. "We know he was here."

"Don't you find it strange that the chart would be here, without the papers?" Casper asked.

"Seems smart actually, that we wouldn't find anything." She tapped her fingers against the top of the chart. "Where would you hide something in a hospital if you were a medical person and wanted the truth to eventually come out about what happened here?"

Casper shuffled his feet and looked around. "Or a bad guy trying to hide what happened. If it's the second group, we're not going to find anything, so let's hope it's the first." He rounded the desk and Ashley followed. There weren't any drawers left in the cabinet to hide anything in. "Guess that's too obvious." He glanced up. "No ceiling tiles."

"You're thinking like an agent. You need to think like a nurse. Nurses were likely responsible for the care of these patients. We need to find the nurses' locker rooms."

After hunting around the floor, Ashley found what she was looking for. Once inside, she faced a wall of very thin, metallic green lockers in different states of being open and closed. Walking closer, she could see some still had garments hanging inside. A nice pair of dress shoes, though the leather was cracked, were still poised perfectly in the bottom of one locker. One sink was present. The other had been torn from the wall—the pipes sticking out like veins from an amputated limb. Much of the tile was missing. In the next section were three stalls with closed shower curtains.

Ashley's skin prickled and she motioned Casper forward. "I just can't be the one who slides those open."

Casper straightened his shoulders and yanked the liners aside like taking a Band-Aid off a wound. He didn't jump back in fright and Ashley exhaled the breath she'd been holding. However, at the third one he paused, something catching his attention. Stepping inside, he grabbed a moldy shower mat and threw it to the side. Then he turned and grabbed a stray pipe that littered the floor and began lightly tapping the base of the shower. Ashley stepped forward cautiously and peered around the curtain.

With the pipe, he motioned around the tile. "I think that mat was hiding something. See how this is scored? It's rough, like someone did it hastily. And at this corner is an opening big enough to fit this."

Casper shimmied the pipe into the gap and the section popped up, flopping to the side. Dust filtered into the air. Ashley stepped next to Casper and peered into the hole. There was enough light to see that there was a box tucked away down there.

A box with "CDC" written across the top in bold black letters.

It resembled her father's handwriting.

THIRTEEN

Casper held his arm out in a warning as Ashley reached forward to grab the package.

"Just a minute," he said.

He bent to his knees. Someone intended for the box to be picked up, as it had a rudimentary strap for a handle fashioned out of duct tape. Motioning Ashley back he picked it up, turned it and set it on the ground away from the shower.

Ashley kneeled next to him, the box in between them. "Do you think it's safe to open?"

Casper shrugged. "It's seemingly meant for government officials to find. I can't guarantee it's not risky, but this is apparently the next clue, so I'm in favor of opening it."

He took a small penknife he'd found in Russell's cabin and sliced through the clear packaging tape that held down the side. The first thing in the box was a stack of papers. Cautiously, he picked them up and handed them to Ashley.

Underneath the stack of papers was another carefully wrapped box with more large black lettering. This time, a few more instructions followed. "Blood Borne Pathogen. Do Not Open. Level IV containment. CDC."

Ashley's eyes widened as she read the notations. Casper slowly closed the flaps. "We're probably fine. Whoever wrapped these seemed to take enough care not to expose whoever found it. They didn't want someone to accidentally contaminate themselves, but we need to hide this somewhere."

"Agreed," Ashley said. She sat cross-legged on the floor and began examining the documents. "These are the medical records for two of the three boys that popped up with the mysterious illness—I guess ES1. They start with the ER evaluation. The date seems to be about ten days after the news article about the balloons that floated into town."

After leafing through the pile, she handed a set to Casper.

"I'll look through the ER records," she said. "You handle the admission notes and the labs for both boys. Might as well use our strengths."

They both read silently for a few minutes. Casper finished the last page and straightened the stack that rested on his legs. Ashley looked at him expectantly.

"You first," Casper said.

"The boys present within one day of each other. First symptoms were classic flu-like etiology. High fever. Headache. Fatigue. Muscle pain and weakness. There is a rash. In one chart, the physician notes that it started on his face and hands."

"That's a classic presentation for smallpox," Casper noted.

Ashley nodded. "After the rash, Patient One is noted to have developed blisters on his trunk, which was what prompted his mother to seek medical attention. The attending doctor, Brent Ward, thought the teen had chicken pox—same with the other boys."

"That confusion would be natural. Admittedly, this ER physician wouldn't be thinking their small town had suffered some kind of biological attack, so viewing this teen's illness as possible chicken pox is reasonable. Assuming the other boys having the same thing would also make sense because of their close proximity to one another, making transmission probable."

"This patient was sent home but then presented two days later when the blisters filled with blood. The doctor also notes strikingly reddened eyes."

"Which are hallmarks of Ebola infection. However, the hemorrhagic vesicles can also be a rare complication of chicken pox, so no real reason to reject the original diagnosis," Casper noted.

"What did you find?" Ashley asked.

"The medical course for Patient One was a very quick demise. Respiratory distress. Bleeding from multiple sites. The lab work is consistent with overwhelming infection. The symptoms described and the signs that the medical team were managing could be consistent with coinfection of both Ebola and smallpox. The teens exhibited patterns of both disease processes."

"So what's next? Where do we go from here?"

"I want to go to the cemetery. Seems like a good place to hide this box. Plus we can see if there was a cluster of other deaths around this time frame."

They walked out of the building and stopped by the car. Casper kept the sheaf of papers and tucked them under the driver's seat. Ashley sat in the passenger seat and he handed her the box. She took it, though with a look of distaste on her face.

Casper drove farther up the hill to the cemetery and passed through its dilapidated wrought iron gates. The dirt roads were largely overgrown with weeds, but it was possible to still make out the twin tracks ground into the dirt where many wheels had passed before. Finally seeing what he was looking for, he stopped and motioned Ashley out of the car, grabbing the same pipe he'd used to unearth the box from the bottom of the shower.

After walking a few steps, he stood before the grave marker. It was one of the teens. Side by side were the boy's parents and likely his sister. The next sets of graves over were the two other teens and their families. Casper calculated the dates in his head. The family deaths were perhaps within two weeks of the index cases. Did that mean the disease had been airborne-spread as smallpox was known to be? Contact-spread like Ebola? Or was it an indication of some combination of both?

Ashley stepped back as Casper began to walk down the line of graves. Each marker held a story of a cluster of deaths this town had suffered within a two-week period.

"Brent Ward. Wasn't he the ER doctor who saw Patient One in the ER?" Casper asked.

"He was," Ashley affirmed.

Casper stood in front of another grave. "And this woman, she was one of the nurses in the medical unit." A heaviness settled over Casper—grief over these innocent lives lost. He kept walking, kept looking. Energy leached from his body with every granite stalwart bearing silent witness to what had come to pass in this town.

"Ashley," Casper called. She walked to where he stood.

The grave marker listed the name Vladimir Sokolov.

Her father's Russian friend—the bioweapons specialist—had died during the outbreak.

What had they been doing?

She reached out and latched onto Casper's hand, her

breath ragged in her chest, apparently needing to feel close to someone other than death.

When those three boys found the balloon on their evening trek—it had led to the deaths of over ten people.

Definitely not chicken pox as the medical professionals initially believed.

Ashley sat silent in the dried grass as Casper hacked away at the ground. She couldn't discern his mood. Angry? Grief stricken? A combination of both? Ever since he'd given her a count of the graves and told her his plan of burying the box that held one of the most lethal bioweapons known to man he hadn't said much to her.

It was cool, slightly breezy. Bearable with a jacket. She could have sat in the car, but she wanted to be there with him. If only to keep him company as he physically exerted himself while dealing with the emotional pain caused by what was no doubt running through his mind.

The clouds rushed by as quickly as her thoughts tumbled through her mind. Seemingly, she couldn't concentrate on one thing. Where was her father? Was he alive? Was her mother still okay? Her brother?

Lord, Casper believes everything has a purpose, but it's hard for me to see that among these stones that mark where innocent people have died by an evil person's hand. What should we do next? Where should we go? If there's an attack coming soon, we need You to reveal the next step we should take to stop it.

Casper neared her, taking the box from her hands and offering her a weak smile. She stood and followed. It fit tightly into the hole he had dug, but the top would be a few inches under the ground. He'd picked a spot at the back of the cemetery at the base of the most distinct tree. He slammed the pipe several times against the tree's trunk, knocking off some of the bark so they could find it again. If anyone happened to walk by, it would be noticeable, but who would ever guess the secret that it held? Who would take that mark as a sign to dig up one of the earth's deadliest threats?

Using his foot, Casper pushed dirt over the box. Ashley helped. Once it was covered, Casper lightly tapped the top, leveling out the dirt. Ashley walked through the markers, picking handfuls of long dried grass. Casper did the same. When they'd gathered enough, they met back up and covered the site with their clippings.

"Hopefully, we'll be able to send the right people to find this. And if we can't, then hopefully the wrong people will never find it."

"What's next?" Ashley asked.

Casper's vision was drawn away from her. He was looking back at the partially burned-out shell of the hospital. She followed his gaze.

Another car—parking at the ambulance entrance just as they had done.

Casper motioned her down. Ashley dropped into a crouched position.

"We can't let them know we've been here," Casper said.

How had Jared found them so quickly? Did he already know about these sites? Even though she could never justify taking a life, they wouldn't be in this predicament if Jared and his men had died. Casper started to crawl. Ashley followed. The distance to the car wasn't great, but within a few feet the palms of her hands were already scratched up from the rough ground. They eased inside. They couldn't see the men by the other car anymore. Casper turned the vehicle on and began to take the road down.

As soon as they hit the paved road, the men came out of the hospital. One pointed straight at them.

"They see us," Ashley said.

Casper took a hard right. Unfortunately, the only way back to the two-lane highway was the small road that passed in front of the hospital.

Too quickly, the other car eased behind them, gaining speed.

"This is going to be rough," Casper said.

Ashley tightened her seat belt. The car swung into the other lane. She looked ahead up the road. A red truck was bearing down on their assailants. Casper hit the brake, and the car veered into their lane just seconds before the beat-up vehicle passed, its horn blaring.

Casper checked the road up ahead and moved into the other lane, quickly speeding up.

"What are you doing?" Ashley asked, her voice an octave higher.

"Getting Jared off our tail." Casper pulled up next to them. "Hold on."

He veered right, ramming their car into their assailants' vehicle. The black car swerved onto the loose gravel shoulder, swiveling violently as the driver tried to get the wheels to find the safety of the pavement once more. The shoulder dropped off, and the car slid off into the embankment. Ashley turned around, saw the car roll one and a half times, settling on its hood.

A haze of dust settled in the air.

Ashley settled back in her seat and looked straight ahead. The jolt awakened the aching in her side.

"Are you okay?" Casper asked.

Ashley swallowed over her beating heart. "Yes. They teach you that in spy school?"

Casper remained silent for miles, constantly checking

in his mirror to see if anyone else was following them. Ashley found herself breathing easier after thirty minutes had passed without seeing anyone suspicious.

They seemed to be in the clear for now.

Casper never had answered her last question. He'd been deathly silent. Was it the incident they'd just survived? Or was something else bothering him?

"I can understand why you're quiet. Is it our pursuers? Or is it finding out about all those innocent deaths in Black Falls? I always need time after the death of a patient to get my bearings, but I'd like to know what you're thinking."

At first, he looked out the driver's window, most likely to hide the emotion on his face. "Seeing those graves is reminding me too much of all the innocent people who are gone because of Jared. My partner died. He was going to find you—to protect you. We'd been working on some intel that was pointing to a pending attack." Casper shook his head in dismay. "This incident that this town suffered happened just over a year ago, but to develop a pathogen like this could easily have taken years…even decades. People in power, those who are supposed to protect us, forget just how patient an enemy can be."

Ashley contemplated his statement. It was true. If there was an imminent attack, it could have been in the works for close to two decades—if her family suddenly being flush with cash was payment for her father's participation in the scheme. Casper didn't think it was possible for her father to do something like that, but if her father loved her as much as Casper proclaimed, then wouldn't he have done anything for her to get the heart surgery she'd needed?

"Even if we stop this, there will always be something

else—someone else bent on destroying everything good about life," Casper said.

A cavernous hole opened up in Ashley's gut. Casper, the über-optimist, was faltering right in front of her eyes. Everyone had a breaking point—a time when they questioned the purpose of life…their purpose. She'd done so herself. Perhaps it wasn't natural for her to always go to God first, but it was for Casper.

"In the ER, I've seen many people suffer devastating injuries. Sometimes, I've had the opportunity to get to know them, to keep in touch with them. All I know is, sometimes going through events like this becomes the glue that binds people together in a way that other events can't," Ashley said.

"It's just the devastation. For the people left behind, I can see what you're saying. We can come to know a different purpose after struggling through traumatic events. Right now, I'm just angry over all that's been lost."

Casper stopped the car and Ashley shifted her focus to the structure right in front of them. Whatever that building had been, it looked like a bomb had leveled it.

And considering their current circumstances, that could be exactly what had happened.

"What is this place?" Ashley asked Casper.

"It's the location of one of the labs that we found in your father's secret files. Guess this isn't going to help us find any clues. If I had to guess, looks like it was destroyed on purpose. Someone is definitely trying to hide their tracks."

Ashley swallowed hard. Who were these people? An entire town decimated from some person's evil plot? Casper was right. It was hard to reason in her mind if they could have anything good come out of these tragedies. What they were seeing was leaving a mark on their lives. Casper's partner and good friend was dead. Her father could easily be gone, as well. Both of them had already nearly died.

Suffering changed a person…that was for sure.

Who would Casper and Ashley be after they survived this?

If they survived this.

FOURTEEN

Casper parked in front of a motel they found in Aspen Ridge, Colorado. According to the files on the thumb drive, this was the other town to have suffered a biological attack of ES1. He paid for two rooms in cash. Both had decided a good night's sleep was warranted. This town was a step up from Black Falls. At least it had people, a sense of life. The cases here hadn't led to the demise of the town.

What had been the difference between the two incidents?

They'd stopped by a thrift shop and bought some up-scale clothes. The next morning, Ashley was already showered and dressed when he awoke. Not that she needed any improvement to her, but Casper was smitten by her in makeup and heels. Both of them had to look professional and not as if they'd been living out of a car for a week.

"I didn't know what I would use this badge for, but I think this is the only way we're going to get our questions answered regarding what might have happened here six months ago." He clipped the CDC badge to his sport coat. "Do I look official?"

"Official enough."

The hospital was close to the motel where they'd stayed the night before. Casper packed everything back into the car. They were considering staying another night, but he thought it best to be prepared.

Just in case they had to run.

After talking to a few of the medical staff, flashing his badge for emphasis, Casper pressed the buzzer for the entrance to the lab.

An older gentleman opened the door. Hopefully, he was here when the event occurred and could give insight as to what type of pathogen might have infected the patients. Many labs sent items out, but this being a regional facility, Casper could see that it looked like they had some decent microbiology equipment on hand.

Casper held his badge up. "I'm Dr. Casper English and this Dr. Drager. I'm from the CDC and we're inquiring about a mysterious illness that hit this area about six months ago."

The man held his hand out. Casper shook it briefly. "Oscar Simmons." He motioned them forward and brought them into a small room that Casper guessed to be their staff lounge. They all took seats.

Casper opened a folder that had a photo of the pathogen. "Have you worked much in microbiology?"

"I have. My whole life."

Finally, they were making headway. Maybe this wouldn't be the obstacle Casper thought it might be. "We know you had patients that showed up with a mysterious illness about six months back. Did you ever identify the pathogen?"

"Two patients. I did not identify the virus. The government did. It surprised me then that no one from the CDC seemed interested despite my phone calls. However, this guy from the military was quick to show up...came in and took things over. Ordered the patients into quarantine and everything. He and his team handled the situation."

"What can you tell us about the illness?" Ashley asked, leaning forward.

"Started out like seemingly every other bad viral illness. High fever. Muscle aches. Headaches. Then they developed a rash that progressed into fluid-filled lesions."

"Did the lesions fill with blood?" Ashley asked.

"They did." Oscar rested back in his chair. "Why are you here now? Has there been another outbreak?"

"No, sir," Casper said. "There have only been a smattering of these cases and we're going back and looking at the data to see what conditions, if any, make the emergence of this virus possible."

"Personally, I don't think it was a natural occurrence, if you know what I mean," Oscar winked.

"What makes you say that?" Ashley asked.

Oscar withdrew his phone from his back pocket and pulled up a photo. "One of the boys had a picture of this." He placed his phone on the table and slid it in Casper's direction.

Casper caught it between his fingers and moved it so it sat between him and Ashley. The skin on his forearms prickled.

It was a photo of a bomblet, the same type and style that fell in Black Falls. There wasn't any feasible way it would have been from the same balloons because of the months between incidents.

"Did your patients come across this item?" Casper asked, handing the phone back to Oscar.

"They did—in the middle of a field. Hard to know if it was part of their becoming sick, but one of the mothers informed the physician about it, who then forwarded it to me. You know what this is?" Oscar asked Casper.

"You seem to have a take," Casper said.

"It's a bomblet. My father worked in a lab during WWII, not far from here, in biological and chemical weapons. War makes governments develop things they might normally leave alone. Desperation causes people to do things they would never normally consider." Oscar tapped the photo. "The first time I ever saw one of these was through my father, who sneaked pictures of them from the facility where he worked. He probably shouldn't have but that's neither here nor there."

"What did your father say they were used for?" Ashley said, trying to focus the man's attention.

"In the photo I saw, these were packed into a warhead that could be launched by a missile and dropped over enemy military. They'd be filled with biological agents. The Soviet Union was quite fond of them, too."

"Do you think the one found by the patient could be left over from your father's work decades ago?" Casper asked.

Oscar shook his head. "Do you see the picture? That thing is new, gleaming shiny metal. No way someone found that in an old building or that it sat in that field for decades. Someone put it there. I don't know who, but it was intentional. Of that I have no doubt."

Casper eased two photos from the folder he'd brought with him. One of Jared Fleming and the other of Ashley's father. They'd been hoping to show these to someone in Black Falls. Hopefully, Oscar would be able to shed some light.

"Do you recognize either of these men?" Casper asked.

"Both of them."

Ashley fell back against her seat, her eyebrows raised. It was almost as if Casper could feel the increased rhythm of her heartbeat in his own chest.

Oscar tapped the first picture. "This is the guy from the military—called himself Jared. He's the one who took everything over. Placed the patients in quickly built bio-hazard units. Even the blood samples had to be processed outside the building. They set up a tent to the back of the hospital for just such purposes."

Casper shuffled his papers. "Did you ever see the pathogen?"

"Only a photo one of my staff showed me."

Casper slid out the photograph of what he knew to be termed ES1.

Oscar slapped the table. "Never thought I'd see that booger again. Hoped I'd never see it. Those two people, I'd never seen anyone sicker in my entire life."

"What happened to them?" Ashley asked.

"The two patients? Alive and well. Still live in town to my knowledge—all because of this man." Oscar pulled Russell's photo closer to him.

"How so?" Casper asked.

Oscar glanced through the partially opened door. Seemingly satisfied that no one was eavesdropping, he leaned forward conspiratorially.

"Not a lot of people know this but one of the ICU nurses told me a man sneaked into the unit one night in one of those fancy suits, and hung a small pouch of fluid on each of these patients. It was late—a few hours after midnight. She was suspicious because she didn't see many of the military types at the bedside overnight. She took a photo of him after he unsuited just in case she'd need to notify the police. I saw that photo. It was him for sure."

"And?" Ashley encouraged him.

"Well, both patients rapidly improved, which sort of quelled the nurse's doubts. Whatever that man gave them, it cured them. I know that with everything in me. However, Jared seemed incensed at the patients' improvement and began grilling the staff, flashing pictures of the man who brought the cure. The nurse confessed she'd seen him—actually feared for her life the man was so angry. After that, they camped out in the ICU undercover and not two nights later they nabbed him."

Casper's gut knotted. If Jared had captured Russell, was he still alive? He reached for Ashley's hand under the table. Her skin was cold, the tendons taut.

"I don't know anything more," Oscar said. "I do still wonder what happened to that doctor—assuming he was a doctor."

Casper gathered up the items, placed them back in the folder and quickly stood. Ashley got up, as well. Did she sense the urgency he was feeling?

Casper extended his hand. "Oscar, you've been very helpful to us today."

Oscar gripped his hand tightly. "My pleasure. Were there other outbreaks other than this one?"

"It's classified." Casper began to guide Ashley to the door.

"You've been a big help, Oscar. Thanks so much," she said.

They exited the staff lounge quickly. One man seemed particularly interested in their presence, his eyes never wavering as they entered the hall.

Outside the lab, Casper pulled Ashley into a small alcove.

Just as they scurried into it, they saw Jared Fleming walk by.

Ashley's heart was in her throat. After seeing Jared, both of them tucked themselves tighter into the corner.

After a few minutes, Ashley saw a housekeeper exit a room just across the hall, pulling a utility cart behind him. She pointed at the partially open door and Casper nodded in agreement.

Casper grabbed Ashley's hand, peeked down both sides of the hall, sprinted into the vacated glorified closet and shut the door behind them.

Ashley leaned against the wall, light-headed. Seeing her father's nemesis again was frightening. A leech they couldn't shake.

"I think one of the people in the lab ratted us out. Jared's probably been hovering in this area hoping we'd check out this site. If I were him, I would do the same thing. It makes sense that we would look into these events. He's probably bribed a few people to let him know if we're seen."

Putting her hands on her legs, Ashley tried to take some slow, deep breaths to ease the dizziness. "How do we get out of here? What do you think Jared would do to us if he caught us?"

Casper smoothed his hand over Ashley's back. She could sense the tenseness in his fingers. He was just as nervous about the situation as she was.

"We have to get back to our car. Once we've done that, we'll hightail it out of here and then try to get somewhere safe for the night. We'll think through the next step."

"We need to get back to the first floor."

Casper nodded. "Stairwells are usually close to the elevators. Those weren't far from the lab."

"Jared's probably in the lab. Don't you think his operatives would be in the stairwell watching?"

"Good point. How do we get on the elevator without drawing a lot of attention?" Casper looked around him. There were several pairs of overalls hanging on hooks that lined the walls. "Quick, we need to get in some of these."

They turned with their backs to one another. The one Ashley grabbed seemed to be for a man taller and heftier than she was. The cuffs ended well past her fingertips. She began to roll them up. Same with the pant legs.

When she turned, she could see the zipper of Casper's pair was taut against his chest. "Seems like we should have picked each other's. We'll have to keep them as is. No time to change." He grabbed two ball caps off the hooks. "Put your hair up inside."

"We look ridiculous. This isn't going to fool anybody."

"It's our best option."

Casper turned around and grabbed the spare utility cart. He handed her some window spray and a cleaning cloth. Opening the door, he surveyed the hall and motioned her forward. The clicking of the wheels over the cracks in the cement sent raw anxiety through her nerves.

They passed a few oblivious people on their way to the elevator and they clamored in as soon as the door opened. Ashley leaned against the wall. She could hardly catch her breath. Would this ruse really work?

The elevator lumbered up the shaft. When the door opened, they saw an armed guard, too paramilitary for hospital security, turned away from them, examining the side parking lot. Jared's crew for sure. Casper rushed out of the elevator, turning to the right so if the guard turned around, he would merely see their backs.

"Keep your eyes forward," Casper ordered.

Ashley's skin crawled with fright. She halted as she saw another armed man in camouflage walking toward them. Casper stopped the cart and opened a sign that read Closed For Cleaning. He quickly nabbed several supplies off the cart and hustled Ashley through the door into the women's bathroom.

No one was inside.

Ashley steadied her nerves by leaning against the wall. "How are we ever going to get out of here?"

Casper bolted the lock and looked around the room. There were a few windows above the toilets in the stalls and he stood on each of them, getting a view of the parking lot. He stepped down and returned to the sinks.

"I'm hoping there aren't very many men. I think there'd only be a small group who would get involved in something this nefarious."

"You're assuming Jared just recruited from the CIA."

Casper scrambled up onto one of the sinks and tested the latch on the window. "That's true. Look at your mind becoming all devious."

It was a stab at humor, but under the circumstances she didn't find it very funny. He stepped down. "You first. I don't see anybody between us and our car. Once you're out the window, just lie on your stomach against the wall a few yards down so I don't land on you. This side of the building is in the shade so you won't be easy to see."

Everything in her wanted to argue, but she didn't see any alternative. Her palms were so sweaty they slipped on the edge of the porcelain sink as she tried to hoist herself up. When she tumbled, Casper caught her.

He gripped her shoulders in his hands. "It's going to be okay. We'll get through this."

Lord, we need Your protection. Guide us and show us a way to make it out alive.

Ashley climbed back onto the sink. With one foot steady on the edge, she reached up and forward, her upper torso through the window, her elbows resting on the sill. Her vision fuzzed. She felt like she was going to pass out.

"Someone's testing the lock," Casper said, his voice resonantly lower. "Cleaning!" Casper hollered.

"We need you to open the door. There is a security concern regarding two fugitives on the hospital grounds."

"Just a minute."

Casper took ahold of each of her ankles in each of his hands and pushed her up and out the window. The cold, damp ground did not cushion her fall. She'd landed haphazardly on her right side and scrambled out of the way just before Casper fell out of the window, too.

They could hear violent blows against the wooden door. Casper scrambled to his feet and held his hand out for Ashley. She didn't register any pain but guessed the adrenaline rush masked whatever might be injured.

Casper stood quickly and ran toward their car. Ashley followed suit. He wrestled the keys out of the custodian's overalls. From the corner of Ashley's eye, another dark-clad figure caught sight of them and ran their way. He raised a sidearm and pelted off one shot.

No sound. He was using a silencer.

It ruptured the metal in the hood of a car just as they ran past.

Ashley reared up, but Casper reached back, grabbed her and pulled her hard. He unlocked the vehicle and they piled in. Just as his key inserted in the lock, another round of shots hit the car.

"Get down!" Casper ordered.

Ashley did as instructed. The car roared back. The back windshield popped like a small explosion. Casper shifted the car into gear, moving forward. Another round popped through the front windshield but didn't take out the window. The wind whistling through the fracture agitated Ashley's already raw nerves.

After several nausea-inducing turns, Casper patted her

gently on the shoulder. She eased up and he continued taking odd, random turns through the town.

"Now where do we go?" Ashley asked.

"We need to stay near this town. This is the last place your father was seen—and was presumably captured. He had a cure that worked. Two of the labs on his list are close to here. We need to check those out. Something tells me that the mystery of all of this ends here."

"How can we do that when people inside the hospital seem to be giving us away?"

"We're not going back to the hospital, but I do have an idea. It's risky."

Casper turned into a shopping mall. "How much cash do we have on hand?"

Ashley shrugged. "Maybe ten thousand."

Casper pulled into a parking spot. "Keep your eyes out for a college-age boy walking to a very beat-up car."

Ashley shrunk down in the seat. Most of the people they saw were women with baby strollers. She was beginning to lose hope when a young man parked in the spot next to them. His car was rusted in several spots. One back passenger window was duct-taped shut.

Casper got out of the car and engaged the man in conversation. Ashley couldn't make out the words. After a few minutes, the young man gave Casper his car keys. Casper opened the back door and began grabbing their belongings.

"We got a deal."

"That easy?" Ashley said.

"When you're a young man looking for an upgrade on your set of wheels, five thousand dollars is a lot of money."

Ashley got out of the car and helped Casper load their stuff into their new wheels. The young man had vanished, evidently escaping with the money before Casper could change his mind.

"What's the plan?" Ashley asked.

"Hide out. Tonight we'll do some reconnaissance on the labs."

Ashley got in the passenger's seat. The car reeked of cigarette smoke.

With Jared on their heels, this plan seemed risky, like walking into the lion's den without any protection.

Did they have any other choice?

FIFTEEN

Casper parked the car approximately a mile away from the lab as marked on the maps found in her father's files. After they hiked through the hilly terrain, he motioned Ashley down into the weeds, where he pulled out a set of binoculars.

Seemingly, he'd been right. Their escapade in leaving the hospital went unnoticed by the local news media. The one radio station that covered the town hadn't had a mention of it. That was surprising considering they'd been shot at in the open daylight. Perhaps no one noticed because of the muted gunfire. Casper reasoned Jared had likely convinced the small local police department, if they'd attempted to become involved, that doing so would put a federal investigation in jeopardy. After all, Jared was still employed by the government.

For Casper, that didn't mean good things. How many people in this town could be under Jared's thumb? Was there a threat that Casper didn't understand? Or was the operation so secretive that it hadn't garnered any local scrutiny?

Through the lenses, Casper looked at the site. There weren't many cars in the parking lot. In fact, just two. An argument could be made that the day shift had ended and they were operating with a skeleton staff, but Casper felt differently. According to the files, this lab had been decommissioned as part of sequestration.

There shouldn't be anyone on-site.

The lab looked like any other nondescript, gray concrete building. No sign called attention to it. There were a few outdoor lights. Outside defenses looked relatively easy to get through. A chain-link fence. No razor wire. But from this distance, it would be hard to tell if the fence was electrified. Casper zeroed in on the one door he could see. It opened and out came two figures. He didn't recognize them.

They were leaving the building unattended—at least that was what it looked like.

"Do you think it's that simple?" Ashley asked as each man got in a car and drove off. Now the parking lot was empty.

"That no one's inside? Maybe. Jared might be convinced we've left the area."

"This seems like it should be our next step. Should we risk going inside?"

Casper rolled onto his back, taking a moment to think. Bright stars filled his vision. It was risky, but what else could they do? Seemingly the men were gone. This could be the place that would hold all the evidence they needed to prove Jared's scheme, to find out where and when the biological attack was taking place, to finally end this nightmare.

This plan worried Casper, but they were also at a dead end. Who could he call? If the town wasn't talking about the incident at the hospital, who knew what powers were keeping this secret or what threat they had in place to keep people quiet?

He turned back to Ashley. "Let's see what Jared's hiding."

* * *

Ashley agreed with Casper's plan to take a wide berth around the building. They approached it from the other side of their observation point. There were a few outdoor lights embedded in the dormer as they grew closer. Casper raised the firearm he had and shot out the lights.

Was this too easy? Did Jared and his henchmen feel so comfortable in their lawlessness that they didn't fear discovery by anyone?

They neared the building under a shield of darkness and slowly made their way around to the door that had released the two men a few hours earlier. Casper shot the lights flanking the entrance, as well as placing a hole in the center of the surveillance camera. The door was held closed by what appeared to be another facial scanner.

Ashley's heart dropped.

"Let's just try it. Your father might be craftier than we think. He's left a trail for us so far. Maybe he left a way for us to get in."

Casper input the same code they used at the cabin. A shield opened up. Ashley set her face on level with the scanner. After a few moments, there was a whir and a faint snap.

Ashley placed her hand on the lever and pulled.

The door opened.

Her fingers tingled as Casper held the door open an inch.

Casper nudged her back and took the flashlight from his pocket. Ashley gripped the door and pulled it back wider. The air drifting out was dank, and Ashley pressed the back of her shirtsleeve to her nose. The stench reminded her of her time in the cadaver lab at medical school—hints of decay with an overwhelming smell of formaldehyde. Though here there was more of a notion of something medicinal.

Seemingly satisfied that the entry was safe, Casper stepped inside the cavernous hall and Ashley followed. The door swooshed closed behind them. Ashley swallowed over the notch in her throat.

The hall was lit with dim red lights. Casper walked forward, reaching behind him for Ashley's hand and she grasped his. Sweat trickled down her back from the humidity. Considering how dry a climate Colorado had, the dense air inside the building seemed strange.

Casper's flashlight bounced from side to side. At the end of the hallway was another door with a lock that resembled the same one on the outside of the building. They repeated the code. Just as before, only a scan of Ashley's face was required for admittance.

The second door opened.

Why was that? All the times before something had been required from Casper, as well.

Ashley's skin pricked.

Casper looked back at her, his eyes narrowed in question. Were they asking themselves the same thing? Each of them had a reason to go on. Did this building hold the secrets to finding Ashley's father? Would Casper get the answers he was looking for about who was responsible for killing his partner? Despite their joint reservations, confirmed by Casper's guarded movements into the next section of the building, they proceeded farther, though Casper's grip on Ashley's fingers tightened—almost uncomfortably.

Once they were through the next doorway, Casper dropped her hand.

Ashley shielded her eyes against the bright lights, blinking rapidly until her pupils constricted to regulate the images she was seeing. Casper turned and they were standing back-to-back at the edge of a circular room.

The first thing Ashley registered was the yellow, tri-circled emblem that denoted they were in the presence of potential biohazards. There were four large rooms, each enclosed with glass. Casper moved forward, Ashley trailing behind him, with the awestruck feeling of a kid seeing an amusement park for the first time.

Except what this building represented wasn't exuberant fun, but death cultured secretly.

Each room was designed to fit a biosafety level—all the way up to level four—which meant they were experimenting with the deadliest pathogens.

"Looks like this lab wasn't decommissioned after all," Casper said.

Any response Ashley thought to say seemed moot. Who was funding this? Casper had made it clear that the United States didn't participate in the development of these weapons anymore—that the Russians had verified it at one point in time. How could that be the case? Two towns having suffered from a frightening, engineered pathogen wasn't a coincidence. Who other than Jared could be behind this? Considering the equipment alone and what it would take to maintain such an operation, this entity had to be requiring millions of dollars.

They kept walking forward. Each room had progressively more equipment. The first room, merely lab tables and microscopes. Little personal protective equipment was in view—things like gowns and face shields. Boxes of gloves lined the wall. Several notebooks sat in a bookcase close to the glass with large black lettering on the binders.

Ashley broke away from Casper and pressed her nose to the window. "Casper, come look at this."

He sidled up next to her. A brief thought flashed into her mind. This is how people viewed newborns in the nursery. Faces up against the glass, breath misting in puffed exhalations, as they looked for their new bundle of joy wrapped in a pink or blue blanket.

Except nothing they were looking at held one ounce of joy.

On the back of each notebook was a letter and a number.

"It's the same code the Russians used for their weapons programs."

Ashley stepped away from the room and walked to the next one. The second room had enclosed hoods. From what Ashley remembered from her brief exposure to infectious disease medicine, level two safety was typically for "mild" infectious diseases. Mild in the sense that they were unlikely to kill the host. Things like measles and hepatitis. A little more caution required but exposure didn't mean death. There was more protective clothing in view. An open cabinet held packaged gowns, face masks and goggles. There was a single door into the room from the hall.

Ashley walked to the next window, stopped and examined the inside of the room. "Casper, maybe we're thinking about this in the wrong way."

Outside this room was a box similar to the facial scanners they'd used to access the building. Controlled access was a requirement of a biosafety level three lab. Also, there were two doors to get in so airflow out could be controlled.

"I've been thinking the same thing," Casper said.

"Jared is working with someone within the Russian government to deploy this bioweapons attack, but why?"

"I don't know if I'd go so far as to make that claim.

Whoever is running this place is definitely using the Russian system, but it could also be a free agent. Someone who wants to cash in on the knowledge he has."

"If we have access to this place, it means my father was here at some point. Do you think he could be aligned with them? That he turned to the other side?"

Casper looked at Ashley, his brown eyes dark as he considered her questions. He closed his eyes tightly and shook his head. "No, I don't believe that—I can't believe it. That you have access to this place...concerns me. This lab's existence on the surface doesn't mean anything nefarious. Perhaps it's funded by a private entity. Perhaps they're researching a cure for ES1 and they have these notes through CIA spies. I don't think we have a smoking gun yet. Maybe your father is helping the good guys and he wanted other good people—" Casper motioned his hand between the two of them "—to find it to help keep it that way. To make sure it stayed in the right hands if he ever went missing. Maybe that's what his files were intended to do."

They passed the fourth room. Now they found the characteristic yellow pressurized suits hanging. The same style Ashley had found torn and discarded in Black Falls. Orange hoses hung from the ceiling.

Casper pointed to a door exiting the circle. "Let's see what's through there."

Ashley followed. As soon as they were through the door, the raucous noises of animals bit into her ear. Metal clanged against metal. As they walked, Ashley identified several different types of animals. Mice. Rabbits. Monkeys.

Some looked listless in their cages. Were Casper and Ashley being exposed to something right now?

Casper turned to his right and stopped abruptly. He

backpedaled, turned on his heel and grabbed Ashley by the shoulder.

"Ashley…"

"What don't you want me to see?"

She pushed past him around the corner. There was a small alcove, and at the end of that alcove sat a man, secured to a chair with leather straps.

Her father.

Adrenaline surged through her body. She rushed forward, but felt Casper's hand briefly try to catch hers.

"Ashley!"

Russell Drager's cry for her wasn't joyful.

It was angry.

She slowed, her heartbeat faltering.

"Go back!" he screamed at her.

The loud pop made her stop in her tracks. There was a loud clang as something metallic clattered against concrete. Ashley looked down.

A bomblet had crashed to the floor and vapors leached from its cracks.

SIXTEEN

Casper's heart sank to his feet as he watched the mist leach from the bomblet. Ashley turned and faced him, tears streaming down her face. He walked toward her and she put her hands up. He kept walking, first reaching out and then easing his hand around hers.

"Casper, get out of here," she said, but he could see in her eyes that she knew the truth.

He pulled her close and hugged her tightly against him. Her body trembled. "It doesn't matter. I've been exposed anyway."

Ashley pushed away from him and ran to her father, falling to her knees and wrapping her arms around him. Russell leaned his head against hers, shushing her like he probably had when she was a child.

Dr. Drager was a faint shadow of how Casper remembered him. Thin—likely malnourished. He'd grown a beard—perhaps not by choice. He wore a ragged pair of jeans that looked half slipped off his hips. His shirt was thin and tight around his torso. The outline of his ribs could be seen easily through the fabric.

Ashley lifted her head up. "How long have you been here?"

Russell narrowed his eyes. A mean look crossed his

face. "You have to leave, Ashley, right now. They'll be coming."

Casper looked around the room for a set of keys for the restraint locks.

"I mean it!"

Ashley stood up and backed away from her father. "We're not leaving without you."

Casper grabbed Ashley's arms. "He's right. This is a trap and we've walked right into it."

Russell looked at him. "The cure, you have to find it, or both of you will die."

"How many days?" Casper asked.

Russell's voice cracked. "Maybe three before you're incapacitated. Go, now!"

Casper pulled Ashley back. She stumbled and fell. Just as he reached down to help her back up he heard the sound of the door opening.

The animals, who had quieted after the sound of the bomblet dropping, were hollering again. Casper looked around. He didn't see any other exit.

Around the corner came Jared and two armed men. Each was dressed in biohazard suits, their weapons trained on Ashley and Casper.

Jared clapped his hands together. The sound was muffled by the thick gloves he wore. "Finally, the family reunion I've been waiting for." He shook a finger at Ashley and Casper. "You two are quite the slippery ones, but I finally accomplished what I was aiming for."

Ashley backed up against a wall and slid to the floor, her head against the wall, her eyes up, blank.

Disbelieving.

Jared walked up to Casper. Evidently, neither the hit he'd taken from Casper's bat nor the grenade had injured him enough to keep him down. As soon as Jared approached, one of the armed men moved closer to Ashley, training his weapon for a kill shot.

"I know what you're thinking, Casper. That if you just put a little tear in my suit, then I'll get exposed and you can have your revenge."

White heat flared in Casper's chest. "You're not even going to deny what you did?"

"Why should I? There's no reason to rebut the truth of what's going on here. You and Ethan discovered that there was a planned bioweapons attack. Ethan suspected I was behind it. Russell already figured out that he couldn't trust me so he developed a cure once he found out my true intentions, which didn't make my partners very happy. That's when I changed my plan."

The other gunman motioned for Casper to place his arms in front of him.

Jared took a step closer. "Come on, Casper, you're one of my smartest agents. Take a look at this picture." Jared opened his arms wide. "What do you make of what's happening?"

"You captured us to flush out the cure. You know that Ashley has been exposed to the pathogen and that her father will give up the location where the cure is stored in order to save her life."

Jared laughed. Casper launched forward and the armed man pistol-whipped him on the back of the head. His vision blackened and he fell flat onto the concrete. The voices became distant, fuzzy.

Stay conscious. Ashley needs you. You can't let her down.

A kick landed to his midsection. His old injuries cried anew.

"Why would I merely allow Russell to cure his daughter? What would that do for me?"

Casper blinked against the darkness. He opened his eyes. Jared leaned over him.

"You want to sell the cure for a price after the weapon is released. You're just in this to make money," Casper said.

Jared laughed. "A lot of money, Casper. A lot." He turned his attention to Russell. "So, Russell, you ready to tell me where that cure might be?"

Ashley could not believe what had happened. Her eyes were closed, and she tried to block out the noise of the men fighting. When they started beating Casper, she tried to crawl to him to get them to stop, but the man who had had the weapon trained on her roughly pushed her against the wall with the bright blue plastic boots that he wore.

Lord, Casper and I need strength and wisdom now. Your purpose cannot be for Jared to win. For him to ransom a cure as he unleashes this terror against innocent people. How can we stop him when Casper and I will be sick?

When we will in all likelihood die.

Ashley contemplated those words and what they meant. Death was usually a surprise for families, even when they were anticipating it. She'd seen this play out time and again in the ER. Even those relatives who helped care for patients in hospice were stunned when the moment came.

We didn't think it would be today. We thought we'd have more time.

Time. That nebulous aspect of life. Always marching forward, never back. Those regrets in life had to be left behind because there was no fixing them, only figuring out how to live with them or move past them.

And now their lives were on the line. The chances of

both of them dying without treatment were high. Was she ready for that? Her thoughts clarified. She understood intellectually Christ dying on the cross. Emotionally, it seemed like a crazy thing to do voluntarily. Die for all of humanity?

Sure, sign me up.

Now, perhaps Ashley gained an understanding of the sacrifice of that situation. Offering oneself so many could be saved. Even if her father gave up the cure, it didn't guarantee that the cure would save everyone infected with ES1. The only way to stop what was happening was to destroy the stockpiles of the weapon and any data on how to manufacture it. Jared seemed determined to find the cure—it was for him the most profitable thing. If they kept it from him, would he give up this attack?

Could they do that before they died?

What was her life worth? A lot if it could save many. Maybe it was her sense of duty as a physician that drove her to defeat death in any way she could. What she knew was that she couldn't live with herself if she didn't do all she could to prevent the demise of millions.

Ashley, resolve strengthening her heart, opened her eyes and looked at her father. His eyes were moist with tears. He seemed to be struggling to deduce the morally acceptable way to handle the situation.

"You can't tell him where the cure is, Dad."

He shook his head against her words. "You don't know what you're asking me to do, Ashley. I can't sign your death warrant."

"Dad, I don't welcome death, but if that's what it takes to stop this man, then it's the only way."

Jared crossed his arms over his chest. "Such an honorable girl you have here, Russell. What you should know is that if you don't give up the cure for Ashley, then I'll go after your wife and son. I'll keep taking out friends and colleagues until you bend to my will."

Fire spread through Ashley's chest. Her vision washed white. She wanted to take her fingers and scratch Jared's eyes out. Casper struggled up onto his hands and knees. He lifted his head, his eyes sorrowful pools of regret. How could they come out of this alive?

"First, being infected with this pathogen might not seem like that big of a deal. If you've had the flu you might even think it's possible to live through it. Then the muscle aches set in. The rash that blisters and fills with blood. The pain is like nothing you can imagine. More than one infected person has chosen to end their own life rather than continuing to deal with the pain."

Casper coughed, sat back on his heels and looked at Russell. "It doesn't matter how terrible it is. I agree with Ashley. I don't want any part of sickening innocents. Jared won't release the weapon without the cure because even he couldn't guarantee he'd survive the pandemic. I'd rather die than see this vile man get anything he wants." If Casper hadn't been a gentleman, he would have spit at Jared's shoes, but his glare was enough even in the absence of the physical act.

Jared walked between Casper and Ashley and placed a hand on Russell's shoulder. "Is this what you want, Russell? To watch your daughter die of ES1—a hybrid of two of the deadliest diseases known to man? Which one will emerge first? The painful lesions of smallpox or the blood—"

"Just stop listening to him!" Ashley screamed.

"The daughter you always wanted to protect…you've now killed. Why you gave her any information is beyond me."

Russell looked up at Jared, trying to shrug his hand

off his shoulder. "I don't know how far your reach is, Jared. Is this really all about money?"

Jared laughed. "Why does everyone look for complicated motives? It can be just about the money. Even you don't know how much foreign entities are willing to pay for a cure. Especially after they see the devastation brought on by the attack."

Russell turned his head away from Jared. The crease lines in his face deepened in anguish. Ashley's heart sank and she reconsidered all of her preconceived notions about her father. It was hard to understand how distance meant love, but in Ashley's father's case, that was exactly what he'd been trying to provide.

Ultimately, he wanted her to live a full life. To protect her from the things he saw—these schemes created by man to kill each other.

And in that realization, she knew he'd give up where the cure was.

"It's in Copper Lake, Utah," Russell said.

Ashley set her face in her hands and wept.

SEVENTEEN

Casper and Ashley were placed in the back of a special transport unit for the drive to Copper Lake. It was necessary for Jared to keep them alive to make sure Russell fulfilled his end of the bargain. That the cure was where Russell said it was. That what Russell delivered eradicated the disease.

And he had two human subjects to test it on to ensure what he sold was the genuine product and not a placebo.

Inside, the vehicle looked like a gutted-out ambulance with protective sheeting. After the doors were closed, Casper stood up and tested the lock. There was no opening it from the inside.

As the hours passed, he could see Ashley start to exhibit symptoms of the disease. Had they made the pathogen even more virulent than when it had hit Black Falls and Aspen Ridge? Had it mutated?

It was possible...even probable.

First came the red flush of fever—just a hint to Ashley's cheeks. She began to shiver uncontrollably; her teeth clattered as she huddled into herself for warmth. The thin sheets that sat on the end of their gurneys provided little warmth, but Casper was glad for it as he didn't want her bundled up trapping more heat.

Ashley lay on her side, her eyes red and rheumy. Her nose began to run, a clear drainage. He left his own thin mattress, sat next to her and placed his lips to her forehead. It was like touching scorched earth.

"How are you feeling?" he asked her, offering a weak smile.

"Not good."

Casper placed his fingers in the groove of her wrist. Her pulse was fast, but strong. Hopefully their captors would be human enough not to let them suffer without some simple medications like Tylenol for her fever. After feeling her pulse, he kept both of his hands around hers. It was like holding a hot, vibrating coal. He closed his eyes and prayed.

Lord, help me find a way to give Ashley the cure. Ashley is strong. She's already lived through so much, but I don't know if she can survive this without help...without Your help. I place myself at Your mercy.

Her voice brought him back. "Why aren't you sick?"

Why aren't I sick?

It was a valid question. He'd been so concerned about her and the quick onset of her symptoms that he'd thought little of himself. It was hard to determine how long they'd been on the road, where mere minutes could seem like hours, but considering the sun was coming up he'd guess at least eight or more hours.

When they looked at the infectious pattern of the other victims, it seemed anyone that came into contact with those showing symptoms came down with the disease. Ashley scratched at her chest. Casper peered closer. The redness wasn't just fever—a rash was blooming on her face and arms.

These symptoms were more aligned with smallpox

infection than Ebola. Evidently the smallpox was winning the emergence fight.

"I was vaccinated for smallpox when I joined the CIA because of the work I was doing. Maybe that's blocking the smallpox effects of the pathogen, which declares itself first. Were you ever vaccinated for smallpox?"

Ashley lifted one scrutinizing eyebrow. Evidently not.

Why wasn't Russell with them? Did they not worry about him getting infected?

"Do you think your dad would have given himself the cure? To protect himself?"

"To see if it worked," was all she could say.

Testing the vaccine on himself? It was against most ethical codes, but it made sense though for the person that Casper knew Russell to be. He was flawed, that was for sure. His sense of protecting his family had distanced him so much from them that they didn't know who he was—his character.

If Russell knew Jared's penchant for releasing this pathogen covertly, he'd have to do the same with the cure. Testing it on himself first seemed like a viable option since the normal research ethics boards weren't available to him. He'd likely done it even before he tested it on the two patients from Aspen Ridge.

"He's immune," Ashley said.

"How does that help us?" Casper massaged his forehead. The blows Jared had delivered to him didn't quite surpass the previous assault by his henchmen, but Casper's growing headache was making it hard to think.

Lord, I need a way out of this with Ashley alive. You placed her in my life for a reason. I was beginning to think it was so that we could be together. Not just for now, not just through this crisis, but for always.

It struck him as funny—how he was developing feel-ings for someone considering the nature of their circumstances. It wasn't dinner and a movie.

It was running from death and mayhem, and not really running...but being caught.

"Leverage," Ashley said.

The word was so soft that the tumultuous noise of his own thoughts almost caused him to miss it.

"What did you say?"

Ashley shifted, her face twisted with pain. Body aches. Muscle soreness. All signs of smallpox...but they could also signify the beginning stages of Ebola. "Jared used leverage to get my father to do what he wanted. We have to get leverage over Jared."

Casper thought about it. Russell gave up the location of the cure because of his love for Ashley. Because he couldn't bear the thought of seeing her suffer and die before his own eyes. What did Jared value more than anything? Power? Status? Position? Those were all givens. What could Casper do at this point in time to threaten those?

Think, Casper. Think. What do you know about Jared? What is it that you want him to do above anything else? I want him to publicly confess this plot. To turn himself in. How do I get him to do that? What can I take that Jared values that is within my control?

Suddenly, the issue became crystal clear.

Jared's life.

Problem was, Casper couldn't kill him, and he'd have to drive him to confession.

The only thing Casper had at his disposal to put Jared into a state of confession was the pathogen he and Ashley were infected with. However, Jared would have to feel the effects of the illness before he'd even consider opening his mouth.

How do I infect Jared before he has access to the cure?

* * *

There was a fire brewing inside of Ashley and the embers grew with each beat of her heart into flames that seemed to be randomly rupturing the cells within her body. A hammer incessantly banged at the inside of her skull. It hurt to open her eyes. The constant motion of the ambulance caused her stomach to roll.

The only comfort was Casper sitting next to her, his hands in nearly constant contact. Checking her temperature, feeling her pulse…simply holding her hand. There had been few instances in her life of a man caring for her in this way. Putting his own comfort aside to do everything he could to ease her suffering.

The lighting in the back of the ambulance was dim. There were no medical supplies, nor were they given anything like water. Ashley's temperature, increased pulse and respiratory rate were adding to her dehydration—none of which would help her fight off the infection.

During her brief glances at Casper, she could see worry and frustration twist his face almost to madness. At times, he had taken to banging on the window that separated the driver from the back compartment to the point where it was exacerbating the jackhammer inside her brain. Oftentimes, she would reach up haphazardly to try to grab his arm to stop the extra noise.

Without her knowing how many hours had passed, the ambulance lurched to a stop. After what seemed like another hour, the back doors opened and cool air brushed against Ashley's skin like a healing salve. Casper released her hand and Ashley tried to sit up, but found the normally simple act impossible.

"Why are we stopping?" Casper asked.

Ashley forced her eyes to focus. Two of the men were standing behind the truck dressed again in their yellow biohazard suits. Something large and orange was tossed into the back of the ambulance, landing squarely on the floor between their two gurneys.

"Make sure she stays alive." Jared's voice.

They only care that I live until they get what they want.

The door closed and she heard a high-pitched zing of a zipper releasing. "What's in there?" Ashley asked.

The first thing Casper showed her was a needle and a syringe. "Everything we need to put my plan into action. First, let's see if we can get you feeling a little bit better."

First thing, he placed a thermometer in her ear. "One hundred five."

No wonder I feel like my skin is on fire. It is.

He took her blood pressure. "Low. Too low."

Her stomach knotted. Low blood pressure could be a sign that the infection had gotten to her bloodstream. Was it possible that it had happened so quickly? It could also be simpler—that she was dehydrated.

A rattling of a pill bottle. Casper rummaged near the top of her bed and found a release that raised her head up. "Take these." Six pills. Two white and four blue. "For the fever."

Her throat was lined with sandpaper. She wanted to refuse them, but knew that battle was futile. Maybe if her temperature came down, she'd be able to help Casper with whatever his plan was. She took the water bottle from his other hand.

One by one, she got the pills down. Each time she swallowed, it felt like she was forcing a pile of rocks into her stomach. Next out of the duffel bag were some IV fluids. Casper unfurled a bright orange strip of plastic and tightened it around her left arm.

Ashley's tongue rolled over her cracked lips. Could any of these things actually help? The death rate associated with smallpox was better than Ebola's, but having both? Was the death rate 100 percent?

My father will stop cooperating if I'm dead.

There was a pinch to her hand and before she knew it Casper had the bag of IV fluids up and hanging.

"I'm going to draw some of your blood into this syringe." He held it up so she could see it. It was one of the smaller sizes, which could hold just a milliliter of fluid.

"Why?"

"I'm going to infect Jared with it."

Ashley shook her head. Had she heard him correctly? "How will that help? We'll be at the place where the cure is and he'll just administer it to himself. That's not going to get us anywhere."

"That's why I have to do it before we get there. If Jared fears death, maybe he'll do what I want him to do. Your father has only given him the location of the cure. If I had to guess, Russell is still keeping some information close to the vest—like maybe he hasn't given Jared the codes for entry."

She started to shiver again as the IV fluids coursed through the veins in her arm. Casper yanked the sheet off his gurney and put it around her.

"What do you want Jared to do?" Ashley asked.

"Make a full confession of his crimes and tell us who is involved in the plot to release the bioweapon."

Ashley laid her head back down and closed her eyes. There was no easy way to say it.

Casper's plan was crazy.

EIGHTEEN

Casper didn't have to guess what Ashley was thinking. The brief, incredulous look in her eyes before she closed them had said it all. The plan was insane. He'd be the first to admit it. The plain truth was that he didn't have any other weapon. If he lunged and tried to break the integrity of the suit, Jared's men could just shoot him on sight.

Whatever he planned to do, he had to draw Jared close to him.

Sunlight faded outside the windows. Casper overanalyzed every sensation of his body. Was his temperature increasing? A constant ache settled into his bones. Was it the pathogen or merely being beaten twice a week? Ashley slept more than she was awake. Every so often, he would nudge her just to make sure she would respond. The IV fluids had helped her heart rate and blood pressure normalize. Her temperature was lower, and her shivering had ceased. For the moment, she looked peaceful.

Over and over, Casper worked the plan through his mind. He was also banking on the fact that Jared would keep Russell from them as he was the only other physician who could offer treatment. He and Ashley hadn't seen Russell this whole journey during their infrequent stops. Just Jared's two goons. Casper's ruse had to be convincing enough to get Jared close to him.

Casper's body rocked as the ambulance turned off the highway, definitely taking a slower pace. It heaved like it was driving over rutted roads and then came to an abrupt stop. Casper lay down on the gurney. This time when the door opened, Jared and his two men stood at the base.

"Get up!" Jared yelled.

Resisting the urge to look at Ashley, Casper opened his eyes. The temperature in the back of the ambulance was sweltering, which aided Casper's plan in making him look ill. He sat up, but then slumped to the floor, wedged between the two gurneys.

"Go get him," Jared ordered.

At each shoulder was a pair of hands. They slid him across the tile and let him fall onto the road. Gravel tore at his skin and he could feel the warm release of blood from the wounds. He'd landed in the best way possible, so that his hand was somewhat pinned next to the pocket that held the syringe.

One of the three men delivered a kick to his back. Gritting his teeth, he remained as still as possible.

"What do you want us to do?" one of them asked.

"Check and make sure he's alive," Jared said.

"He was warm when we touched him," the other noted.

A rush of exhaled air punctuated the coming night. "He could still be dead," Jared said.

Casper slid his fingers to the top part of his pocket and gripped the plunger of the syringe. As he pulled it out, he gently unsettled the cap so the needle was exposed.

A man, who Casper hoped would be Jared, settled an arm on his hip and shoulder. Just as he was turned onto his back, Casper opened his eyes, confirmed it was Jared under the biohazard suit, arced his arm until the needle buried itself into Jared's shoulder and injected the contents of the syringe. He heard a satisfying hiss of air leaking from the puncture site.

Jared scrambled away from Casper clutching his arm. "What did you do?" he screamed. His cohorts reached for their sidearms.

Never had Casper seen armed men draw in biohazard suits. It was like some funky science fiction Western, but they were quick and Casper held his hands up in surrender, the syringe visible in one of his hands. "Only what you did to us." Casper threw the syringe at his feet. "Infected you with whatever you infected us with. I'm guessing your dual pathogen called ES1."

Jared motioned for one of his goons to pick up the syringe. They wouldn't go near it.

"It's Ashley's blood," Casper said.

Jared marched forward and picked it up.

Casper got up to his feet. "Ever been vaccinated against smallpox, Jared?"

The two men kept weapons trained on Casper. "Actually, I have been."

"Then my guess is that you have some time before you begin feeling just as bad as Ashley."

"You think I'm going to take your word for this?" He brought the syringe close to Casper's face. "This joke you've played is going to do nothing more than hasten your death sentence."

"That is...if it was a ruse. I assure you, it wasn't."

"Well, we'll see. Go in and get Ashley up. It's time to see what her father's been hiding."

Casper turned around and entered the back of the ambulance. He disconnected the bag of IV fluid that had been running, but kept the IV in place. Gently, he picked up her small frame and rested her on his shoulder, stepping back onto the ground.

When he turned and took the building in, his heart fell. What he'd imagined would contain the stockpile for the cure would be a massive warehouse. What stood before him was nothing more than a house in the middle of the desert. A large house, but still.

As he turned, one of the men pressed the tip of his gun into Casper's back. Russell waited with the door open. As Casper passed it, he saw another facial scanner to the side that Russell used to gain access. Once inside the house, Russell weaved through a couple of small passageways until he came to a staircase. At the bottom of the brittle wooden steps was another door, a punch code lock to the side.

Once that opened up, everything about Casper's impression of the facility changed.

Underneath that simple house was a fully functioning lab and medical suite. How had Russell gotten the money to fund this? Was he working with someone? Or was it from the original sum Jared had given him? Casper hoped Russell had an ally…someone they could trust. Maybe that someone could help them. Then it dawned on him. Vladimir had likely been his confidant. They'd likely worked together on the cure, and that was probably why he was dead.

Russell motioned them to a bank of rooms and slid one of the glass doors open. Casper rested Ashley on the bed and connected her to the small portable monitor that sat there. Jared stomped into the room and pulled the hood off his head. Casper didn't regard that as the wisest of moves considering Jared didn't know if what Casper had told him was the truth or a lie. At Jared's command, the two gunmen hustled Russell into the room, as well. Then again, anger made men do irrational things.

Jared held up the syringe examining its contents in

the bright light. "How long will it take you to test this for ES1?" he asked Russell.

Even from Casper's position, he could see the blood inside. Evidently this was enough to convince Jared of the veracity of his statement.

"You're assuming I have a test and the lab equipment to run it, which I don't," Russell said.

Jared threw the syringe across the room and turned on his heel, his breath seething through clenched teeth. He wrestled out of the remainder of his suit, sweat causing his shirt to cling to his skin. His hands were clenched into tight reddened fists.

Casper put the oxygen probe on Ashley's finger. She moaned intermittently. At least she was responsive. The rash on her body had begun to blister and the fluid looked pink tinged. The discoloration could signify that she was suffering the effects of both illnesses.

Her oxygen level was borderline low.

Just as Casper reached for an oxygen mask, Jared threw him against the wall. Even though the man had at least thirty years on him, the force with which Casper hit stunned him. His head snapped against the brick and he almost slipped to the floor, his body numb, disoriented from the surprise assault. Stiffening his legs, he pushed himself up. More than anything else, he didn't want to look weak in front of this man anymore. He was tired of being chased by this maniac. It was time for his evil deeds to be exposed.

Casper had to get himself, Ashley and her father out of this alive. As far as he knew, they were the only ones who knew about the pending attack now that Ethan was dead.

"Just what exactly was your plan with this stunt?" Jared asked, spit on his lips.

Casper narrowed his eyes. "How long ago was your

smallpox vaccine? You know, it's been shown that they wear off after a few decades. And who knows if it would have worked against what you've paid someone to create."

Jared spun his head around and eyed Russell. "You don't have to look too far to find who the creator of ES1 is."

The trio of yelling men pulled Ashley from her fever-induced delirium. She was in a room…a small medical area that resembled the setup of her own ER rooms. Something was attached to her finger and she pulled at it haphazardly, not quite able to register in her mind what the common piece of medical equipment was.

Physically, she felt eviscerated. Her nerves were on fire. Her tongue—thick, hot and dry. She'd give anything for an ice chip, although she'd need buckets to ease this thirst. Each small movement of her body caused pain. Her skin itched and when she ran her fingers over her neck to scratch, she felt small raised areas.

Blisters.

The disease was progressing rapidly—like flames over dry, barren land. What she'd said before about being at peace with death had upended itself now that her body pummeled toward that reality.

Lord, bring me peace. I'm scared. I've never been this sick. I don't want to die. I want a life… I don't want to be alone anymore.

Upon opening her eyes, she'd awakened unto a movie already half over. Casper thrown against the wall by Jared, whose arm was dangerously close to his throat before Casper fell and righted himself. Phrases she couldn't understand. Jared was out of his biohazard suit. The two armed gunmen stood off in the distance—way off—even though they still had their suits in place, but they held their weapons with much less conviction than before. In fact, they were mouthing something to one another and Ashley thought she saw the word *go* silently uttered several times.

Casper muscled his way past Jared and went to Ashley's bedside. "How are you feeling?"

Now she realized how inane a question that really was to someone flirting with death. She gave him an unconvincing smile. It amazed her that he still looked so well. He released a lever and eased her bed up. She'd heard the last several exchanges, but nothing made sense in her mind.

Casper's face hardened. He was angry and looking directly at her father. "I want to know what Jared's talking about."

Her father's features looked markedly aged even compared to a day ago. He reached his hand out, grabbed a chair on rollers, eased himself down and buried his face in his hands. "Jared is right. I took the work that the Russians had started and finished it. I manufactured mass quantities of ES1."

It felt like she was falling. Her heart raced. The room tilted violently, and she pressed her fingers against her temples to give her mind a steadying hand.

Jared walked to the bottom of Ashley's bed. "Makes you think differently about a man, doesn't it?"

Ashley avoided Jared's glare and looked up at the ceiling. She sank back against the mattress. Even Casper's face looked crestfallen at the news. The man he'd admired his whole adult life had just face-planted off the pillar Casper had built for him and all he was left with was chunks of plaster in his hands.

"How could you?" Casper asked, his voice cracking.

"Do you know how many people died in Black Falls? Over ten! That's probably only the beginning."

Russell straightened himself up into the chair and rolled closer to Ashley's bedside. "I know you will never understand my decision at this time in your life, but I did it to save you. We needed money to pay for your heart surgery. Jared assured me it was sanctioned by the US government. I thought the amount of money he provided proved that to be true."

Ashley's mind drew a blank. She didn't have enough experience with world-upending confessions to offer him any type of statement. Should it be an angry tongue-lashing? Words of comfort? Even she didn't know how she felt toward her father. The mixture of his absences, of them finally finding him, collided within her like atoms splitting. Between this illness and these revelations—her mind…her body fractured.

"I knew then it was wrong even if sanctioned by the government. Solving a short-term problem this way has ruined my life and many others. The reason I left over two years ago was to find a cure for what I'd created."

Casper seemed as paralyzed as Ashley.

Russell turned to Jared. "What you don't know, Jared… is that Ashley is yours. You infected your own daughter."

Ashley's mouth dropped open. How was that even possible?

Jared doubled over, placing his hands on his knees, gripping them until his fingers washed white. When he stood, the veins in his forehead jutted out. His face had gone purple with rage. "It's not true!" he yelled.

Jared stalked up to one of his henchman and ripped the sidearm from his hand. He paced back to Russell and pressed it against temple.

Russell calmly held his hands up in silent surrender.

Every one of them stilled in the room for endless minutes. Would this be the end? Would Jared shoot everyone?

"In your heart you know it's true, Jared, but denial is a powerful thing. When you found out about Ashley's mother's pregnancy…you left her, calling her a liar. I merely picked up the pieces. We both loved her. I just won out, but mostly because you gave up. That's why I hid what Ashley looked like from you for all those years."

Jared eased his weapon down.

Casper crossed his arms over his chest. "Putting the family dynamics aside, you have a problem on your hands. You're going to get just as sick as Ashley if you don't get the cure, but I won't allow Russell to give you the cure until you tell us the exact time and date of this bioweapons attack and you confess to these other crimes."

Jared laughed. "No, you *do not* dictate to me what I will do. The first thing we're going to do is make sure the cure Russell has really works. Show me where it is."

Jared and Russell left the room, leaving Casper and Ashley alone. Even the two gunmen momentarily disappeared. What threat was Casper? It was obvious he wasn't going to leave.

They couldn't escape with Ashley in her current state.

Casper rounded the bed and sat down, taking Ashley's hand. "I don't…I don't even know what to say. This isn't over. I will get us out of this…all of us…alive."

The first thing she felt was bitterness. Casper, the ultimate optimist, was painting a reality she didn't believe in. The reality she'd known all of her life was a fairy tale. If what Russell said was true—and really, why would he lie—then who was she? The daughter of an evil, maniacal man?

Ashley withdrew her hand from Casper's and rolled away from him. Her body was swept with heat again, and she tucked herself tightly into a ball from the rigors. Her muscles seized up, racked with pain.

All she could do was cry and scream silently in her mind.

Casper laid a comforting hand on her shoulder. Even though the weight of it increased her pain, she found that she needed him. Needed something sure. Needed his presence.

He was the first man who hadn't abandoned her despite grim circumstances.

If there was any good to come from Russell's confession, it was that she understood a lot that had happened in her life. Now, everything her father had sent her over the past months strangely made sense. The pieces clicked into place. Her mother and Jared had been an item. The pictures her father had sent her proved it. The photo of Jared and her mother staring lovingly into one another's eyes was proof of something more than friendship. Her instincts had been correct.

Personally, she'd never felt that way toward a man. Not until Casper.

And now she was going to die before she knew what being loved by a man truly felt like.

NINETEEN

Russell returned with three bags of solution in his arms and plopped them down on the counter next to Casper. Jared raised the gun up to Russell's head. "Step back."

Russell did as instructed.

To Casper, Jared said, "Pick which one you want to give to Ashley."

Clearly, Russell raising Ashley and hiding her identity from Jared had been a wise choice because after this act there wasn't any way that it could be claimed Jared had a compassionate bone in his body. This was an interesting game Jared played. If Russell had given him bags of something other than the cure, then Ashley could get sicker or even die. Even though Russell's actions were suspect, he'd at least demonstrated that he loved his daughter by trying to fix his mistake in developing a cure for ES1.

That was why Casper felt all of them were a cure and it really wasn't a hard choice. But what did that mean? Russell was likely immune from already treating himself in the past. If he wasn't, he wasn't demonstrating any worry about it.

These three doses were for him, Ashley and Jared.

Russell was giving the cure to Jared without getting

anything in return. Casper's plan could be ruined—only Jared's suspicion kept it alive.

Casper picked one from the group and held it up.

"Great," Jared said. "Now put it back down and pick another one."

This game could go on forever, but Casper picked up another bag.

"Now infuse it," Jared ordered.

Casper looked to Russell for advice.

"The infusion runs over twelve hours," Russell instructed.

Ashley still had her IV in place. Casper looked through the cabinets until he found some IV tubing. He primed the set and after several false starts, he loaded the cartridge into the pump and started the infusion to run over the stated time.

Casper looked at Jared just as Jared slumped to the ground. For a few moments, Russell and Casper looked at one another, perplexed, and both seemed to be running through the same conversation in their minds. *Do we help him or do we take advantage of this opportunity to escape?*

"Help him!" one of the gunmen ordered.

Cautiously, they walked to the fallen man. They bent down, hoisted him up and carried him to the bed on the other side of the room. Even without a thermometer, Casper could feel Jared's temperature was high.

So fast? Even for Ashley it took a few hours. Jared shivered. Casper measured his temperature with a thermometer affixed to the wall. Elevated. Just like Ashley's.

"Why do you think Jared was affected so quickly by the exposure?" Casper asked Russell.

Russell busied himself by slipping an oxygen sensor onto Jared's finger and then turned the monitor on.

"Jared has a medical condition that has left him immunocompromised."

"What is it?"

"He doesn't have a spleen. It was taken out after he suffered an IED attack in Iraq. The point is, he doesn't have an adequate immune system to mount a defense. These dual pathogens are going to kill him faster than any other victim so far."

Jared moaned and opened his eyes. "Didn't you just violate patient confidentiality?"

Russell crossed his arms over his chest. "I'm not your doctor. We're hostages. I'm not sure that particular law applies here."

Casper reached behind him for an IV start kit. "Are you going to let us put this in and give you the cure?"

"Not for the price you ask. I'll have my gunmen shoot you first."

"Then I guess we wait," Russell said, stepping back from the bed.

From the cabinet, Casper reached in and got a bottle of Tylenol and ran the faucet to fill a cup of water. Once he had both, he held them out to Jared. "Better take these. It's about to get rough."

As an unknown amount of time passed, all Ashley was aware of was the percolating battle within her. Pain cramped her muscles. When she turned to find comfort, agony zinged through her nerve endings. Her only reprieve was the cool washcloths placed on her forehead and tender kisses to her hands.

Everything was hazy. Tunnel-like. Figures at the end she couldn't reach. Speaking was impossible with her teeth clenched against the agony. There were words being spoken to her, but they sounded engulfed in water.

Then, the words slowly began to make sense. Her right hand was enclosed in the comforting grip of two others. A forehead pressed to her forearm.

A prayer being whispered for her…by Casper.

"Lord, heal Ashley from this sickness. You brought her into my life for a reason. It can't have been just to die. Is she the one for me? I feel like we're meant for each other. Give us the chance for a life together. Help me find a way to save her just as You saved us."

Did Casper mean for her to hear those words? This repeated mantra became the focal point of the comfort she could most count on, something she could believe in, wrap her heart around. She had mused these things in her own mind and now she knew that Casper felt the same way.

When she was able to open her eyes, the room was dim. There was a rattle of a stool toppling over, but she was too tired to startle. Casper's face popped into view, a broad smile consumed with relief welcoming her back.

He hugged her gently. "How do you feel?"

Shifting in the bed, she sat up. The room spun wildly and she gripped the side rail to slow things down. Taking stock of her symptoms, she felt most had decreased in severity. The headache was nearly gone. Muscle pain tolerable. She touched her chest—the blisters were resolving.

She looked at Casper standing next to her and he had an IV in his arm with an infusion going. "How do you feel?"

"I think having a recent smallpox vaccine kept most of the symptoms at bay. Your father's cure did the trick and brought you back to me."

It was strange hearing those words…*your father*. Even if Russell had been what she thought of as a good dad, he wasn't her father biologically. Jared hadn't denied his confession. Russell had adopted her, raised her and, though imperfect, had loved her in the best way he could. He'd sacrificed for her—his distance had been meant to keep her safe.

Adoption. Sacrifice. Were these things really different from what God did? Jesus had done these things for her. Firming that up in her mind made the things Casper talked about more reasonable. Sensible.

True.

Maybe all these things had happened for a reason.

"Casper—"

"Don't say anything now." He raised the head of the gurney so she could sit supported. "We can talk about things when we're out of here."

Ashley looked past Casper and saw Jared lying on the other bed in the room. He shook violently, his skin red and blistering. His moaning caused her head to dip between her shoulders. "You haven't given him the cure yet?"

Casper sat down. "Why would we? He hasn't fulfilled his end of the deal. If he doesn't confess then I don't think we have enough evidence to prove what he's done. What are a few pictures and files? Your father's statement will be viewed as corrupted considering what he's done. Jared will weasel out of this, Ashley. He's been smart enough to hide his fingerprints."

"Where's my father?"

"Sleeping."

"I know you're not going to like what I'm about to say," Ashley said.

"Don't even think of asking me what you're going to."

"Then I won't, but just do it."

Casper stood. The stool rolled away—violently ejected. It veered into Jared's gurney. He didn't even wince.

"We don't owe him anything, Ashley. He's suffering because of his own evil plan. He'll twist this around and make it look like we're the criminals. We'll go to jail. He'll be out and rich. This is what you want?"

What she wanted was not to give a man a death sentence for not cooperating. There had to be a better way than to impose the same type of madness that men had used for centuries.

"You're better than this, Casper. I am, too. If you believe God orchestrated these events then there has to be a way for the truth to win without coercion. There has to be a path where mercy works."

Casper gripped the IV pole in his hand, staring at her. His eyes darted about the room as if he were searching for a counterargument and coming up blank.

"Russell's not going to agree to this."

Ashley pulled her knees up and laced her arms around her legs. "My father doesn't have to. We're the only other two people in this room and we have everything we need to give it to him. Please, Casper. Could you look back on letting this man die and truly be at peace with it? You're a doctor. You swore to never do a patient harm. I think you want to be with me. I want to be with a man who will uphold the oaths that he takes."

"He's...a criminal."

"He's still a person, too. Maybe the one thing that can turn him around and get him to confess is showing him grace. Jared could be the way he is because no one has ever done that for him before. He's just used to people treating him like you are and doing the same to others."

"What you're asking me to do... I just...can't."

And with those words, Casper walked out of the room.

TWENTY

Casper stalked into the next room and lay down on the only available gurney. This room was similar to the one Ashley and Jared currently resided in. Russell slept next to him and didn't stir when he entered. The gunmen were nowhere to be found. Russell had checked outside, and the two vehicles were gone. So far, the communications equipment Casper had found had been disabled—likely by Jared for this very reason. None of them could walk for hours in this desert to try to find help. They'd have to find a way to communicate from the site. At least they had access to food and water. There was a video camera they'd found that was Casper's only hope of documenting Jared's confession.

Now it all seemed like folly.

The anger Casper felt wasn't because Ashley was wrong... It was because she was right and he didn't want to confess to himself the lengths he had gone to torture someone else. Jared was definitely in the throes of the illness and had gotten there much more rapidly than Ashley. He would quickly progress to death without the cure.

Casper clenched his fists. The IV pump connected to him rang off that the infusion was complete, and he angrily yanked the line out, pressing his thumb to stem the small flow of blood. Ashley's infusion had finished a few hours earlier. Clearly, she was better. Giving the cure to their enemy? He tossed and turned for another hour, unable to come to any other conclusion then what Ashley had offered. He whipped the sheet off his body and walked back to the room that held Ashley and Jared.

Ashley was sitting next to Jared doing the same things Casper had done for her. Washcloths were placed over his forehead and around his neck.

Her head was bent. She was praying...for Jared...the man who'd thought nothing of trying to kill them—on more than one occasion.

Casper cleared his throat to draw her attention. She looked up, but didn't move from her spot. He walked to the counter and picked up the last dose of Russell's miracle concoction.

"I'm glad you changed your mind," Ashley said.

Casper straightened out Jared's arms and pulled a tourniquet taut around his upper arm. He swabbed the area roughly with an alcohol patch.

"I don't know if I've changed my mind," Casper said. "I only agree with what you said. I don't know if I'd ever have peace again if I let him die when I could save his life."

He grabbed the IV and shoved the needle into Jared's arm. Jared didn't respond to the pain. Blood flowed out and Casper put the adapter in place. His chest was tight. His pulse raced. Everything in him argued against this... about how stupid it was. At how they had just given their captor exactly what he wanted.

They'd given up their leverage.

Mostly, he was mad at himself for not feeling better about doing this. The difference between God and man became a clear division in his mind. It proved to him that he couldn't perform this action on his own. A power was working through him because he would not have delivered this cure without it.

He connected Jared to the cure and set the pump for twelve hours. After watching the IV site for a few minutes, deciding the infusion was going into the vein, he straightened up and looked at Ashley.

She was crying. "Thank you," she said.

Guilt washed over him. If Casper told Ashley what he was thinking…there wasn't any way she would ever love him. "I'm going to check on Russell." He turned on his heel and had walked to the door when he heard her voice stop him.

"Casper, wait."

He laid his hand on the door, but couldn't turn to face her. In some ways, he felt like giving Jared the cure had killed them all. If not now, then when this bioweapons attack took place. They still didn't know when it would happen. All of their goals would remain unrealized and people's lives were at stake.

"I know that was hard," Ashley said. "You've done more for me than any other man and…I love you."

His heart leaped to his throat and his hand gripped the frame of the door harder. Waves of emotion pounded in his chest. Something in him kept him from turning around. He didn't want this moment to happen in front of his enemy. Casper did care for Ashley—deeply—but was he ready to say those words?

"No matter what happens I just wanted you to know that."

Her words comforted him. There was a pull in him—her mind begging him to turn around, and his own desire to return the words she had said to him.

Not now. This wasn't the right time. He hoped she

would understand his distance because there were so many things to tell her that he just couldn't bring himself to say right now.

Ashley's voice softened. "Maybe when Jared's better, he'll change his mind about things. That's all we can hope for." Disappointment tinged her words. Because he'd not said anything, she was changing the subject. His heart dissolved in a pool at his feet. He'd crushed her.

Maybe Jared would change his mind. Probably not. Hope had a long way to come.

After about six hours, Jared started turning the corner. His skin was markedly cooler under Ashley's touch. Intermittently, his eyes would focus, staring at her intently, before succumbing to sleep once again.

How would things end? Seemingly, she was closer now to finding out than a few hours ago. Changing a hardened heart was not easy. Could she change Jared's mind? Were these actions of his spurned by jealousy? Money combined with jealousy? Was that all it took to take innocent lives?

People had killed for less.

Casper and Russell peeked in on them intermittently, but otherwise left Ashley and Jared alone. They were attempting to get some form of communications established. Evidently, no cars had been left behind when the gunmen deserted Jared. Ashley felt like there was a way Jared could reach out, so they were dependent on him.

Ashley took the time to pray. It had worked for Casper and couldn't hurt anything, but the words felt foreign to her. She could definitely see how her own relationship with her father influenced the way she felt about God. Was that fair? Had she really let God into her life wholeheartedly—without reservation? Had she ever made up her mind to focus on Him and surrender her life to His control? Ultimately, no.

Now was the time.

Two more hours passed and Jared all of a sudden struggled to sit up. Ashley helped him and offered him sips of water. He had difficulty looking at her, but she wasn't going to step away from his bedside. Not until they had a little conversation. In hopes that would happen, Ashley turned on the video recorder and set it underneath the gurney.

Becoming attuned to Ashley's steadfastness and perhaps realizing that he didn't have gunmen to threaten them with, Jared turned toward her and studied her for the longest time. What she didn't want was to start the conversation—she wanted to let him take the lead. Perhaps if he didn't feel pushed he would be more inclined to Casper's plan.

"I would never have been a good father to you. When your mother told me about her pregnancy, I literally ran away to another county and then spent my life convincing myself she had lied to me to trap me into a life I didn't want."

Ashley put herself in her mother's shoes, trying to imagine how she'd feel if the same thing had happened to her. Her mother was barely nineteen when she became pregnant. The father disappearing with no intention of providing support.

"Russell and I had been vying for her attention and she gave in to me. We always had this competition between us and I wanted to win no matter what—no matter what the fallout was."

Ashley pulled away from him slightly. "Is this really the man you want to be? Bent on destruction no matter what the cost?"

"In the case of your mother, it was easy. I knew Russell loved her and he had the fortitude to raise a child not blood related as his own."

Heat fumed in Ashley's chest. There were good men who made bad choices with evil consequences. Her father was solidly in that category. Then there were just evil men, a description that fit Jared like a glove.

"I made some decisions where the money I got from this deal would erase away all potential consequences. I could flee the country and live the kind of life *I wanted*."

"People died, Jared. You released ES1 intentionally in two different populations."

"Your father always felt guilty about bringing that pathogen to life…but he still manufactured it. The money he got paid for your heart operation, your big house— also funded his ability to build this and make the cure. Russell taking that payment allowed you to live the lifestyle you grew accustomed to."

Blood money. She'd gone to medical school and it had been paid for by the dirtiest of currency. How could her father do that? How could he leave her with this mental burden? Both Russell and Jared had committed crimes… horrid crimes. Her father creating that virus had led to all these events. He wasn't an innocent man.

"You were the one who decided to release ES1. To see if it worked."

"That's true. After I released the pathogen the first time, all those deaths caused your father to break. Unlike me, Russell has a moral code, though it might have veered off course for a long time. Before I released the pathogen, I later realized, he was already working on a cure, but the realization that the pathogen was so lethal pushed him even harder to develop a cure behind my back. I found that out in Aspen Ridge after he cured those two patients."

Ashley fingered the scar—a remnant from her surgery. Could she blame him? Would she make the same choice if faced with an ill child? Even if her child were dying, she couldn't see creating something that could kill so many.

Jared continued. "After Russell sneaked in and cured those patients, my plan changed. I realized a cure was more valuable than the pathogen itself. Desperate people will do anything and pay nearly any price to live. Just as your father chose to take the money I offered him when he found out you needed heart surgery. Because of Russell, I even had evidence the cure worked. Foreign entities would require proof. They're not going to pay billions for a placebo. I put deals in place. A US attack that used ES1 would panic the rest of the world. As soon as the US figured out there was a cure, I was counting on them to pay me for it."

"So, you'll confess to all this on tape?"

He laughed and slapped the bed rail with his hand. "Such a sense of humor. No, this was merely for you, Ashley, as consolation for not doing what I should have done as your father. Of course, I'll deny every part of this. The only one likely to face prison time is your father."

Ashley bent down and picked up the tape. "I don't think that's true." She clicked off the video recorder and rewound it enough to play back a portion of their conversation. At hearing his own confession, Jared lunged at her. The glass doors to the room crashed open. Just as Jared began climbing over the bed rails, Casper made a dash toward the bed, went airborne and pinned Jared to the gurney. Russell quickly followed with a roll of duct tape. They bound Jared's hands and feet together.

"Just in the nick of time, too," Casper said. "We've managed to repair the radios and secure communications with the FBI and Homeland Security since we don't know exactly who you've corrupted within the CIA."

Jared screamed…a blood-curdling, agonizing scream. Perhaps he realized they had so much more than a confession. When the entities he worked with realized he wouldn't be holding up his end of the bargain, they'd kill him.

Ashley picked up the tape and walked out of the room.

TWENTY-ONE

Casper didn't know what day it was. They'd been down in the bunker perhaps two days. The sun was just coming up. Ashley looked past him through the windows at the back of the trailer. He leaned over and tried to catch her gaze but she just tilted away from him again.

They were in the back of a specialized biohazard unit. Casper didn't blame their rescuers. Until it could be verified that neither he nor Ashley were sick it was the safest precaution. It would take a long time to sort out what had happened between Jared and Russell over the years—exactly who all the players were. Both would face prison time for sure, but maybe Russell would get some leniency for trying to do the right thing in the end. Even though his choices were bad ones, he had ended up saving lives.

Casper reached out and settled his hand over Ashley's. She gripped the gurney tighter and he slowly tried to lift up her fingers. His heartbeat edged up as he wondered if she would engage in conversation with him.

"I made a mistake that I need to correct," Casper said.

Ashley released her hand and he took it between both of his, working his thumbs over the back, massaging it gently. His fingers tingled touching hers. Even in their current state of disarray after being on the run for over a week, she was stunningly beautiful. When Casper's memory returned, he knew he'd fallen in love with her long before she even knew he existed. He'd watched her from afar, silently hoping that someday she would notice him.

Not under these circumstances, but God did work in mysterious ways.

"You said something to me…and I didn't say the right words back," Casper confessed. "It didn't feel like the right time to me."

Ashley's blue eyes locked on his. Their matted tiredness glistened.

Casper pulled her hand and rested it against his chest. "I have loved you longer than you've known me. Your father's stories bonded me to you. I hoped for a day when we would find one another—although not due to such a crisis, but it worked."

God worked.

"I love you, Ashley Drager. I want to spend the rest of my life with you. I'll give up my work just to spend every moment with you…if you'll have me."

Ashley's eyes smiled and she leaned forward.

Their lips met and it was the sweetest kiss Casper had ever experienced.

EPILOGUE

Ashley held Casper's hand as the ultrasound tech guided the wand over her gelled belly and her right thumb and index finger twirled her wedding ring on her left hand. Both of them had decided that waiting to start their lives together considering all that had happened would be the most foolish choice of all. If they had learned anything, it was how precious life was and on what a thin thread it dangled.

The images popped up on the monitor and Ashley's heart swelled. She could see the heartbeat fluttering. It seemed strong and normal to her but who was she to know what these gray-and-black images represented? Being an ER doctor didn't mean she was adept at interpreting fetal ultrasounds.

Ashley reached up and caressed Casper's face, and he leaned down and kissed her on the lips. Even after a year of marriage, the tingle in her toes at his touch remained.

So much had happened. Once Jared had realized that they'd recorded his confession and had been too weak to overpower the three of them, he'd surrendered and confessed where the attack was going to take place. Federal investigators also found supporting proof in the car recovered in Aspen Ridge, where Casper and Ashley had stowed the hospital documents. They'd even managed to find the buried blood samples from Jared's first planned outbreak. Jared also told Casper where Ethan's body was so he could be returned to his family for burial. Considering Russell had fashioned a cure, he was given a lighter sentence, but would still remain in prison for the next decade.

Russell would miss seeing his grandson grow up. Miss all the important developmental milestones.

"I'm happy to say that the heart structures appear normal," their doctor said. "Of course, we'll have to wait until the actual delivery to know for sure, but I don't think you two should worry."

That was the best information she was going to get any doctor to give her at this stage in her pregnancy. Ashley reached and pulled Casper down, clutching him tightly.

"I told you his heart would be just as perfect as yours is," Casper said.

She smiled through the tears. It was true. Her heart was perfect now. It had been mechanically repaired a long time ago, but now—with Casper's love and a renewed love of God—it was whole. The two gaping holes once present had been filled by all the right things.

"I told you, Ashley, God is always working for good."

* * * * *

If you enjoyed FUGITIVE SPY, look for these other books by Jordyn Redwood:

FRACTURED MEMORY
TAKEN HOSTAGE

Dear Reader,

Fugitive Spy was inspired by Ken Alibek's nonfiction book called *Biohazard*, where he documents his work with the Soviet Union creating and stockpiling biological weapons of mass destruction.

The concepts in this book might seem unbelievable, but they are pulled from factual accounts. The video described by Casper and Ashley of Gruinard Island exists and can easily be found on the internet. Unit 731 was real as well as Operation Cherry Blossom. Many elements of the novel are based on real-life events. However, if I can ease your mind some, to my knowledge there is not currently a bioweapon called ES1 or one that combines smallpox and Ebola. Let's hope and pray that never happens.

What is clear from Mr. Alibek's book is that some governments have made the choice to operate outside the law when it comes to chemical and biological weapons. My impression from him from the book is that we shouldn't let a piece of paper (as in a law) satisfy our intellect that countries are always operating inside the law without some form of verification.

I always LOVE to hear from readers and will be particularly interested in your thoughts on this book. I can be reached via email at jordyn@jordynredwood.com or by mail at the following address: Jordyn Redwood, PO Box 1142, Parker, CO 80134.

May good men always shine light to uncover the darkness.

Many blessings,
Jordyn

Get 2 Free Books,
Plus 2 Free Gifts—
just for trying the Reader Service!

SPECIAL EXCERPT FROM

Love Inspired
SUSPENSE

*A serial killer is on the loose on a military base—
can the Military K-9 Unit track him down?*

*Read on for a sneak preview of
MISSION TO PROTECT by* Terri Reed,
*the first book in the brand-new
MILITARY K-9 UNIT miniseries,
available April 2018 from Love Inspired Suspense!*

Staff Sergeant Felicity Monroe jerked awake to the fading sound of her own scream echoing through her head. Sweat drenched her nightshirt. The pounding of her heart hurt in her chest, making bile rise to burn her throat. Darkness surrounded her.

Where was she? Fear locked on and wouldn't let go. Panic fluttered at the edge of her mind.

Her breathing slowed. She wiped at the wet tears on her cheeks and shook away the fear and panic.

She filled her lungs with several deep breaths and sought the clock across the room on the dresser.

The clock's red glow was blocked by the silhouette of a person looming at the end of her bed.

Someone was in her room!

Full-fledged panic jackknifed through her, jolting her system into action. She rolled to the side of the bed and landed soundlessly on the floor. With one hand, she reached for the switch on the bedside table lamp while her other hand reached for the baseball bat she kept under the bed.

Holding the bat up with her right hand, she flicked on the light. A warm glow dispelled the shadows and revealed she was alone. Or was she?

She searched the house, turning on every light. No one was there.

She frowned and worked to calm her racing pulse.

Back in her bedroom, her gaze landed on the clock. Wait a minute. It was turned to face the wall. A shiver of unease racked her body. The red numbers had been facing the bed when she'd retired last night. She was convinced of it.

And her dresser drawers were slightly open. She peeked inside. Her clothes were mussed as if someone had rummaged through them.

What was going on?

Noises outside the bedroom window startled her. It was too early for most people to be up on a Sunday morning. She pushed aside the room-darkening curtain. The first faint rays of sunlight marched over the Texas horizon with hues of gold, orange and pink.

And provided enough light for Felicity to see a parade of dogs running loose along Base Boulevard. It could only be the dogs from the K-9 training center.

Stunned, her stomach clenched. Someone had literally let the dogs out. All of them, by the looks of it.

Don't miss
MISSION TO PROTECT by Terri Reed,
available April 2018 wherever
Love Inspired® Suspense books and ebooks are sold.

www.LoveInspired.com

Looking for inspiration in tales
of hope, faith and heartfelt romance?

Check out **Love Inspired**® and
Love Inspired® **Suspense** books!

New books available every month!

CONNECT WITH US AT:

Harlequin.com/Community

Facebook.com/HarlequinBooks

Twitter.com/HarlequinBooks

Instagram.com/HarlequinBooks

Pinterest.com/HarlequinBooks

ReaderService.com

Love Inspired®

*Ten years ago, Jeremiah Weaver left his Amish
community to become a navy SEAL. Now that he's back,
can he convince the woman he left behind—widow and
mother of two Ava Jane Graber—that he's here to stay?*

*Read on for a sneak preview of
THEIR AMISH REUNION,
by Lenora Worth,
available April 2018 from Love Inspired!*

"What are you doing here, Jeremiah?"

"I didn't want you to see me yet," he tried to explain.

"Too late." She adjusted her *kapp* with shaking hands.
"I need to go."

"Please, don't," he said. "I'm not going to bother you.
I…I saw you and I didn't have time to—"

"To leave again?" she asked, her tone full of more venom
than he could ever imagine coming from such a sweet soul.

"I'm not leaving," he said. "I've come back to Campton
Creek to help my family. But I had planned on coming to pay
you and Jacob a visit, to let you know that…I understand
how things are. You're married—"

"I'm a widow now," she blurted, two bright spots
forming on her cheeks. "I have to get my children home."

Kneeling, she tried to pick up her groceries, but his
hand on her arm stopped her. Jeremiah took the torn bag
and placed the thread, spices and canned goods inside the
bottom, the feel of sticky honey on his fingers merging with
the memory of her dainty arm. But the shock of her words

made him numb with regret.

I'm a widow now.

"I'm sorry," Jeremiah said in a whisper. "Beth never told me."

"You couldn't be reached."

Ah, so Beth had tried but he'd been on a mission.

"I wish I'd known. I'm so sorry."

Ava Jane kept her eyes downcast while she tried to gather the rest of her groceries and toss them into the torn bag.

"Here you go," he said, while her news echoed through his mind. "I'll go inside and get something to clean the honey."

Their eyes met as his hand brushed over hers.

A rush of deep longing shot through her eyes, jagged and fractured, and hit Jeremiah straight in his heart.

Ava Jane recoiled and stood. *"Denke."*

Then she turned and hurried toward the buggy. Just before she got inside, she pivoted back to give him one last glaring appraisal. "I wonder why you came back at all."

He watched as she got into the buggy and sat for a moment. Without a backward glance, Ava Jane held her head high. Then Jeremiah asked for a wet mop to clean the stains from the sidewalk. He only wished he could clean away the stains inside of his heart.

And just like her, he wondered why he'd returned to Campton Creek.

Don't miss
THEIR AMISH REUNION by Lenora Worth,
available April 2018 wherever
Love Inspired® books and ebooks are sold.

www.LoveInspired.com